A Thug's Redemption 3

The Wrath of Andre

A Novel By

Yani

With the Russian Mob on his heels and the crooked Philly Police putting him in an impossible situation, Jamal has no choice but to revert back to his street mentality ways if he wishes to keep breathing. Unable to trust his fellow officers or determine who is a friend or foe, Jamal forms a deadly alliance with a man more ruthless and deadly than he. Presumed dead for more than twenty years, Andre is back bringing a hail of bullets and leaving a trail of bodies in the EXPLOSIVE finale to this series.

Yani

A Thug's Redemption 3: The Wrath of Andre

By Yani

Published by Anitbeet Productions

Copyright © 2013 by Yani

ISBN 978-0996966610

Printed in the U.S.A:

Dedication

I want to dedicate this book to my eager readers of the A Thug's Redemption series. This is indeed the grand finale; there will not be a fourth. My childhood friend, and former neighbor, Tiffany Williams, as well as Cherell and Shawanna Whitfield; the three of you showed so much enthusiasm with these books and helped spread the word to others letting them know that this is THEE book series to read right now. Thanks so much for the support and for the shout outs on Facebook, Twitter and Instagram. I truly appreciate it. Again, I have to shout out my partner in crime, Bryheem "Turtle" Bryant. Your letters and words of encouragement kept me grounded and preserved my sanity at a time when I swore I was losing it. Thanks homie. Of course I have to shout out my mother, the all famous Betty Bunns. Every day that I sell a book, I hope I continue to make you proud. And lastly to my children, Destiny and Demetrius: Let my work ethic inspire you to be greater than what I aspire to be. This is a lesson I will continuously reiterate to you every day I am allowed to breathe. I do this for the both of you. There would be no me without the two of you.

1

Denise tossed and turned, unable to sleep, sick with worry over her youngest son, Braheem. This was the third night that he hadn't come home and despite what her husband and his father Norman told her, she was tempted to call the police and fill out a missing person's report.

Out of their five children, Braheem was by far their biggest disappointment and their greatest challenge. Despite the fact that he was an academic student while in grade school and came up in a well-rounded family and grew up in a middle class section of West Oak-Lane, Braheem let the pressures of his peers, the streets and the deceitful glamorous lifestyle that came with it, slowly suck the life out of him.

Braheem was a junky. There was no denying it. The signs had been there for a long time but during the last couple of years, it had gotten worse. The missing money from Denise's purse, the stolen electronics, the way his appearance had slowly started to diminish as well as the rumors, whispers and chatter from her neighbors talking about seeing Braheem around the Morton Homes on Haines Street and near Waterview Recreation Center buying from local drug dealers, were more than enough to conclude that her baby-boy was a junky. Denise just didn't want to believe it. But her son's erratic behavior and his last act of thievery; stealing her wedding ring after she accidentally left it on the kitchen counter when she took it off to wash the dinner dishes, was making it sink in. Her son was a drug addict. But there had to be something that she could do. Norman suggested they wash their hands of him, as they had already done all that they could to help him.

Denise stirred a little more and accidentally kicked her husband. He shifted in the bed unable to sleep with all of her movement and put his arm around her.

"What's wrong, baby?" Norman asked his wife.

Denise sighed and looked at her husband in the darkness. "I'm sorry, I didn't mean to wake you," she apologized.

"It's okay. I wasn't sleep. What's the problem?"

"I'm really worried about Braheem, Norm…" Denise started.

Norman groaned and shook his head. "Denise, we've been through this too many times."

"I know," Denise replied. "But he's our son, Norman. It must be something we can do to help him. He's been gone for three days. Something could be wrong!"

"It's not a matter of something could be wrong. Something IS wrong. He's a got-damn junky, running around here robbing us fucking blind to shoot that shit in his arm or snort it. He's beyond help. I've had enough. You should be tired of his shit by now. I know I am," Norman said acidly.

"How can you say that?" Denise shook her head as her eyes became teary.

"Did you find your wedding ring?" Norman asked her. He waited for her to respond knowing that she wouldn't. When she didn't, he shook his head in disgust. "I'm changing the locks first thing in the morning."

"Norman, no!" Denise pleaded. "Please, he's our son."

"Don't debate me, woman. My mind is made up. I've had enough! Sometimes you have to realize when a person is beyond help. You can't help a person who doesn't want to be helped and doesn't have the got-damn sense to help himself. He's a grown man. We raised him right. We did the best we could to keep him away from the streets and he chose. He chose! And now we have to choose. When a baby bird reaches its maturity, the mother bird pushes him out the nest. That bird can choose to either spread its wings and fly or crash and burn. Braheem has to make the same choice."

Denise was quiet for a moment letting her husband's words sink in. "But what happens if our son can't fly. I don't want to have to bury our child, Norman!"

Norman took his wife by the hand and kissed it tenderly. "Let's hope it doesn't come to that."

Earlier that evening, Braheem walked into a back room of a house in South Philadelphia. He waited eagerly for his supplier Marcus to join him so he could cop his dope and get high. He was strung out and doing anything short of sucking dick to get his daily fix. Morality and rationality had gone out of the window after he stole from his parents the very first time. He never expected it to go this far. What started as him taking a few sniffs at a party with a few friends spiraled out of control and turned him into a full blown dope fiend.

Braheem could have had a great life. He previously was extremely handsome with walnut colored skin that held a natural glow; big, round, dreamy chestnut colored eyes and full lips that hid a mischievous and seductive grin. But the constant chase for dope caused him to neglect his appearance and he was looking very much so like a junky.

He fidgeted, rubbing his neck and looked around the room. Out of habit, he began to plot on what he could steal and how much he could get for it for his next fix.

At times, Braheem wanted to get away from the life. He wanted to get clean and reclaim his life to make himself proud and to make his parents proud as well. He hated the way he was hurting his mother and the way he disappointed his father. But it was hard to break away. The preverbal monkey was already on his back and had a hold of his soul.

Braheem heard a door open and close behind him. He turned to see if it was Marcus that had finally come to join him. But it wasn't Marcus. Instead, it was an older white man. He was dressed in a silk white shirt with the top three buttons undone exposing the curly hairs on his chest. Braheem could see a scar that stretched across the front of his neck as if he had been the victim of an attempted throat slashing. A gold chain dangled around his neck with a cross hanging on the end. He coupled his silk shirt with an equally expensive pair of off-black slacks and polished his outfit off with a shiny pair of black colored, wing tipped shoes. Though his hair was a mixture of silver and black giving him a salt and pepper look, his mustache and beard were jet black and his tiny eyes were equally dark. He looked intimidating and Braheem was immediately shaken.

"What's up?" Braheem spoke timidly. "I was waiting on Marcus."

The mysterious man adjusted the gold Rolex on his wrist. "Oh, I had him run a few errands for me."

"Oh," Braheem said, disappointed. "He had something for me. But I can come back later."

"I know. You're Braheem, correct?" the mysterious man asked. Braheem could hear a hint of an accent in his voice but couldn't tell if it was Russian or something else.

"Yeah, yeah. I'm Braheem," he replied quickly.

The mysterious man stuck his hand out to be shaken. "The name is Kristoff. But you can call me Alek." Kristoff replied with a mischievous grin that shook Braheem to his core. Braheem shook his hand hesitantly. Kristoff walked over to a desk and reached inside. He then pulled out a small off-white package of dope. Braheem looked at it and immediately became aroused, eager to get his hands on the package to get his fix. He licked his lips as his palms began to sweat.

"I understand you have something for Marcus?" Kristoff asked.

Braheem looked from the package that Kristoff played with in his hands feeling like he was in a trance and met Kristoff's glare before looking back at the package. "Yea…yes. I um, I'm a little short cash wise but I told him I had a ring that's worth at least two G's." Braheem stammered.

Kristoff was quiet for a moment. He was used to junkies coming in trying to wheel and deal or barter for their next get high. "Let me see it."

Braheem reached in his jacket pocket to retrieve his mother's stolen wedding ring that he had wrapped in a napkin and handed it to Kristoff. Kristoff was sure to take it in the napkin, not wanting to get his finger prints on it. He looked it over expressionless before wrapping it back in the napkin and tucking it in his back pocket.

"You've been a loyal customer of Marcus for a long time. Come back to me in a few days and I'll have a job for you," Kristoff said as he handed the package of dope to Braheem.

Braheem took the package quickly with a shaking hand and stuffed it in his jacket pocket. "Thanks, man. I really appreciate it," he said as he backed away. He left the room almost bumping into another man that was coming in. He excused himself and left out quickly.

"I thought you were going to cancel that junky nigger," the guy said after he closed the door.

"I just did. He'll be dead before the end of the night."

"What about the other nigger? No sign of him yet?"

"No, but he'll show up again very soon. With the right motivation of course. And when he does, his black ass is going to wish he stayed dead." Kristoff twirled the cross that dangled around his neck

between his fingers as he thought of Andre Williams.
He wanted him dead more than anything in the world.

Not long after Norman and Denise had finished their conversation and were trying to go back to sleep, they heard the front door open and close downstairs. They both listened as their estranged son made his way upstairs.

Norman shook his head in disgust and flung the sheets back so he could get out of bed. Denise grabbed his arm to stop him."

"Please, at least let him get a good night's sleep," she whispered.

"He's not sleeping under my roof another got-damn night, Denise I mean it. If he stays, I go. Now something has to give."

"That's not fair, Norm!"

"It's your choice, Denise." Norman said firmly.

Denise searched her husband's face. She didn't need to see what was hidden in the darkness to know that he was dead serious. "Then let me talk to him. At least let me try to talk some sense into him first."

"By all means, all the good it'll do. Be my guest," Norman said as he folded his hands behind his head.

Denise got up from the bed and put her house robe on. She clicked on the lamp that stood on her night stand and made her way over to her bedroom door. "Please God," she whispered with her eyes closed as she took a deep breath. She opened the bedroom door just as Braheem had reached the top of the stairs.

"Braheem…" Denise started.

"Hey mom," he replied in a low voice.

"We need to have a serious talk about what's going on with you."

"What do you mean? There's nothing going on. If you're talking about me being gone the last couple of days, I just figured I'd give you and pop a break and get out of y'all way," Braheem replied.

"No, I'm talking about your drug abuse. You can lie about it and deny it all you want but we know. We know, son. And we've known for a while."

Braheem interrupted his mother, "Mom, don't start. Please, I'm tired and I really just want to get some sleep."

"Braheem, we want to get you some help."

Yani

"Can't this wait until the morning? I said I'm tired," Braheem said loudly. He really just wanted a moment's peace so he could enjoy his package of dope. He hadn't even gotten his high yet and she was already blowing it.

"Don't you raise your voice at me!" Denise snapped at her son.

Braheem took a deep breath and tried to calm himself. "I'm sorry, mom. I didn't mean to yell. I'm just really tired. We can talk. Can I just run to the bathroom real quick?"

Denise nodded and Braheem made his escape into the bathroom, closing and locking the door behind him. Denise leaned into the wall rehearsing in her head what she was going to say to her son. She prayed that this was going to be the breakthrough that was needed. She heard her son shuffling around in the bathroom and then the faucet water turn on. She thought she heard him sniffing and leaned against the door to listen closely. She heard a sniff and then another sniff as her son was feeding the dope up one nostril and then another.

Denise knocked on the door rapidly as her heart raced. She twisted the door knob, trying to gain access but to no avail. She couldn't believe her baby was getting high in her bathroom.

"Just a sec, mom. I'll be right out," Braheem said as he felt the drug begin to take over. He took deep breaths as he began feeling the drug's effects.

"Braheem! Open this door right now! Open it, damn it!" Denise shouted. Norman listened from the bedroom and shook his head. He tried to warn his wife that there was no reasoning with their son now, but she didn't want to listen. He decided to wait before kicking in the bathroom door and kicking his son's ass in hopes that finally Denise would see things his way.

Braheem opened his mouth to reply but felt short winded. He suddenly felt as though he was suffocating and his heart rate sped up rapidly. He felt hot as though his insides were on fire and his body began to writhe and jerk violently back and forth. He gagged and choked, reaching for something to grab onto to steady himself. He tore the curtains from the shower almost falling into the tub. His chest heaved as he tried taking a breath to call to his mother for help. He then fell back onto the toilet, snatching down the curtains from the window and knocking down the knick-knacks that were adorning the bathroom walls. He finally managed to let out a piteous howl as blood dripped from his nose and flew from his mouth.

Denise heard the commotion in the bathroom. "Braheem! Braheem!" Denise screamed as she banged on the door. "What's happening? Answer me, Braheem! Braheem!" She banged on the door in extreme panic mode, knowing her son was in trouble and praying he wasn't over dosing. "Norman!" she screamed for her husband. "Norman, get in here! Do something!"

Norman jumped from the bed and ran to the bathroom. He listened and heard his son gagging and sounding as though he was under a violent attack. He rammed on the door with all of his might. Finally, the door gave way and they could see Braheem writhing on the floor as blood poured from his nose and mouth. His eyes stared wildly at the ceiling as his back arched repeatedly. Denise screamed in horror as she watched her son suffer from a violent overdose from supped up heroin. Norman dropped to the floor and held his son, trying to control his body movements.

"Do something! Help him, God please. PLEASE!!" Denise begged and prayed as she watched, feeling helpless.

ATR 3: The Wrath of Andre

Slowly the back arching stopped and Braheem trembled and shook in his father's arms. He whimpered and groaned softly before he finally stopped and took one last breath.

Norman looked his son over and shook him. "Braheem?" he said as he shook him again. "Braheem… son… Braheem?!" His son lay in his arms, lifeless and limp. Norman pulled him close and cried.

"No, no Norman. Not my son. Not my baby!" Denise pleaded as the tears flowed heavily from her eyes. She rushed back to her room and snatched the cordless phone from its cradle before frantically dialing 9-11.

When the ambulance arrived, they tried reviving Braheem but there were no vitals. He was pronounced dead on the scene. They placed him in a body bag and sent him to the morgue to do a full autopsy seeing right away that his death was a possible homicide.

Denise sat at her dining room table with her husband next to her. He put his arm around her and she rested her head on his shoulder, weeping helplessly. A detective came over to them.

"Are you the parents?" the detective asked. Denise was unable to speak so Norman nodded his head.

"Yes, we're his parents," Norman said.

"I know this is hard but, I just have a few questions. Are you up for this now or would you rather wait?"

"No, let's do it now and get it over with," Norman replied.

"It appears your son has succumbed to a drug overdose. Were you aware of his drug usage or was this the first time that you knew of it?" the detective asked.

"We had our suspicions because of his behavior and the rumors. Sometimes people would come to us and tell us but we never knew for sure," Denise said in a trembling voice.

"What do you mean by his behavior? Was he acting differently?"

"Well, yes. Some money was turning up missing. Things around the house like my iPad, one of my cell phones, the stereo in his bedroom and a few other things," Denise replied.

"And your wedding ring," Norman reminded her.

ATR 3: The Wrath of Andre

The detective jotted down what was told to him. "Were any of these items reported stolen? Was a police report filed?"

"Well, no because he's our son. We thought that maybe we could talk to him and get him some help," Denise said defensively as she wiped her face with a tissue.

The detective waited a moment before asking more questions. "The people who were telling you that they saw your son, did they ever say if they saw who he purchased from?"

"No," Norman replied becoming frustrated. "What does this have to do with anything?"

"Well sir, judging by the nature of your son's overdose, it's quite possible that he was given something stronger than normal to cause this to be as violent as it was. If we can track down his supplier, maybe we can determine whether or not this was intentional or an accident," the detective explained. "Did your son have any enemies or do you have any names of friends that we can talk to that may know a little more about his activities than you do?"

"He never brought his friends here. But I took his phone after…" Denise hesitated not wanting to say that her son died. She took a deep breath to compose herself. "…before you all got here, I took his phone. It fell from his pocket."

"If you don't mind, we would like to take a look at it to see who he talked to last to help us find out what happened to your son and who's responsible. Whatever it was that he used, we definitely need to get it off the streets as soon as possible to make sure this doesn't happen to anyone else." The Detective closed his notepad and tucked it inside of his pocket.

Denise retrieved the phone from her house robe's pocket and gave it to the detective.

"Are you trying to say that my boy was murdered?" Norman asked.

"Well, we won't know for sure until the autopsy comes back. While we wait for toxicology reports, we can work other areas to see if maybe your son owed money to a dealer or maybe had some kind of beef on the streets with anyone. Either way, we'll do our best to get to the bottom of this."

Norman sat quietly for a moment. Denise could tell by the look on his face that something was wrong. They waited until the police finished their investigation and left from their home. Denise was locking the front door when she heard Norman talking in the kitchen. She stood in the dining room and listened.

"Hey Jamal, sorry to call so late. You got a minute?"

"How're you doing, Uncle Norm? Is everything okay?" Jamal asked as he looked at his watch on his night stand and saw that it was almost 2AM.

"Have you heard anything else about Samir's murder? Do the cops have any leads on…" he trailed off for a minute. "Do they know who that is in the photos they took from his security cameras?" Norman whispered into the phone.

Jamal sat up in his bed quietly not wanting to wake his new girlfriend, Tiffany. "No one's really said anything to me. I'm not sure if they are dragging their feet because they're glad he's dead or if they're keeping quiet because they know something. Uncle Norm, what's going on?"

"Braheem is dead," Norman said, becoming choked up. "He overdosed in our bathroom. The detective thinks maybe the dope was too strong but isn't sure if it was intentional or an accident."

Jamal's heart raced. He was well aware of his baby cousin's drug habit and had once tried talking to him to no avail. He had a feeling that something like this was going to happen but he was hoping that he was wrong. He rubbed his hand over his face and shook his head in sorrow. "Damn Unc, I'm so sorry to hear that. How's Aunt Denise holding up?"

"She's hanging in there. Listen, I need to see you as soon as you have some time."

"Let me throw some clothes on. I'll be there in about twenty minutes."

"Thanks Jamal." Norman hung his phone up and put his hands to his face. He shook his head in part anger and in part sorrow. If his son had been murdered then he knew it wasn't because of money owed or because of something that was stolen. He and Jamal weren't the only ones who recognized Andre in that photo. Someone was retaliating and made an example out of his son. But why? Norman wondered. Were they trying to send a message?

He heard the floor squeak and turned around to see his wife standing behind him. He motioned for her to come to him and wrapped his arms around her when she did.

"Why did you call Jamal?" she asked him. "And what does Samir's murder have to do with Braheem?"

"I don't know," Norman lied. "Just a hunch. You know when anything goes down with that bastard and then something happens in this family, I always feel like he's responsible."

"Yeah, but he's been dead for more than three months. He didn't do this."

Norman remained silent not wanting to tell his wife too much. If their son had been targeted because his brother was alive and took out Samir, there was no telling if this was simply an eye for an eye or if more was coming. His heart raced as his thoughts began to wander.

"What aren't you telling me, Norm?" his wife asked as she let him go and searched his face.

"There's nothing to tell," Norman shrugged his shoulders. "I guess Samir can still affect me even from the grave." He kissed his wife and walked her upstairs to their bedroom. He insisted that she went to sleep even though she felt that she wouldn't be able to. But after a few short moments, she cried herself to sleep.

Norman went back downstairs and stood in his doorway, waiting for Jamal to arrive. When he pulled up in his new 2013 Infiniti, Norman quietly shut the door behind him and went to sit in his nephew's car.

"This is nice. What made you trade in the Impala?" Norman asked as he looked at the detail of the car.

Jamal shrugged, "The Impala was from 2009. I just wanted something more up to date. When I saw this at the Philly Auto Show, I knew I had to cop one." Norman nodded his head. They were silent for a moment. "So what's up, Unc?"

Norman waited a moment before speaking. "I saw your father," he said quietly.

"What!? When?" Jamal replied as his heart raced. He never said anything to his mother but brought the photos from Samir's surveillance to his uncle for a second opinion. He wanted to make sure his mind wasn't playing tricks on him. Norman confirmed that it was his brother, Jamal's father.

"About a month ago. I came home from work one day and he was sitting in my living room. I thought I was going to have a fucking heart attack."

"Why didn't you say something?" Jamal asked.

"And risk having my brother locked up for doing what we're all glad somebody finally did? I wasn't about to turn my brother in. Fuck that."

"Uncle Norm, you know better than anyone that I wouldn't have given him up to 5-0," Jamal looked his Uncle over. "He's really alive?"

Norman nodded his head. "Yes…but he's different…cold…"

"But why? How?" Jamal asked, confused.

"It's a long story. All I can tell you is some special unit higher than IAB helped him fake his death. From what he said, they told him it was the only way they could focus on Kristoff and some of the others who were on the take. Andre knew Kristoff was coming for him because of what happened with Smitty in prison. They gave him some kind of vest to wear where if he were to get shot, the vest would burst looking as if he were bleeding. Andre said he never anticipated that Samir would be the one to shoot him. He said for years he wanted to kill that fucker. But the unit who he was working for had him on bullshit assignments all the way in California away from Kristoff, Samir and everything that was happening here. When he found out what happened with your girlfriend and your daughter, that's when he made his way back. And that's when he learned of everything that was going on and how Samir damn near had you and Shawn caught up in a drug war. Cops were thinking that Samir or the Columbians who were moving in on his territory were the ones taking cops out along with some of the street niggas. It wasn't either of them. It was Andre. From what he said, he didn't realize Samir had protection all the way up to IAB which is why no matter how much he tried to make the evidence fall on Samir, he always walked away clean.

"When he took you that night that Shawn killed your girlfriend, that's when Andre had enough and he killed him. He said he did it because he knew Samir would keep coming for you and he wasn't about to give him another chance. He's been watching us for a while. He's been watching you for a while." Norman trailed off.

Jamal shook his head as he tried to take in everything that was being told to him. "Where is my father now?" he asked his uncle.

"I don't know. He only reached out to me that one time. He said he would be in touch but I haven't heard from him. But I'm telling you Jamal, my son didn't overdose by accident. He was killed on purpose. I don't know if this is an eye for eye retaliation and they're on some vindictive shit because Samir is dead or…"

They both fell silent as if they came to the same conclusion but didn't want to speak on it.

"I'ma see what I can find out on my end. Give my condolences to Aunt Denise. Let her know if y'all need anything, I got y'all without a problem," Jamal said.

"You watch your back out here," Norman warned his nephew. "Something about this doesn't feel right. And with Samir dead, who knows where this could be coming from."

"Unc…did Braheem have any kids?"

"Yeah, he has a three year old son, Brandon. Sometimes his mom brings him over so we can spend time with him. I'll call her tomorrow to let her know what happened. I know Denise is going to want to be closer to Brandon now especially with what just happened."

"Yeah…" Jamal said softly as he thought of his younger cousin. He shook his head. "I'ma call you tomorrow Unc, as soon as I find anything out about Braheem and I'll see if I can pull up information on Samir's case also."

Yani

"Thanks. Text me when you get in. I'ma try to get a little sleep. This week is about to be a damn mess." Norman shook his nephew's hand and climbed from his car. He stood in his doorway and watched him pull off before going in the house and locking his door. He never noticed the car that pulled off, following behind Jamal.

2

Jamal drove back to his apartment with his cousin Braheem, on his mind. He began to think what possible connection he could have to Samir's murder and the fact that his father Andre resurfaced and undoubtedly killed Samir. He wondered if it was something his uncle wasn't telling him.

When he got to his apartment, he noticed the bedroom light was on. He was hoping that he had returned home before Tiffany had awakened.

"Hey, I thought you would've still been sleep when I got back in," Jamal said as he hung his jacket up. Tiffany was lying across the bed reading a book. She took her glasses off and looked up at him when he gave her a kiss. "I woke up to turn the heat down and noticed you were gone. I figured the station called you in so I decided to just wait up for you," she searched his face and saw that something was troubling him. "Are you okay?" she asked.

Yani

Jamal sighed and sat on the bed next to her, staring blankly at the wall. "My uncle called me. My cousin Braheem overdosed on heroin in their bathroom."

Tiffany sat up in their bed. "Aw babe, I'm sorry to hear that! Is he okay?" she asked as she caressed the side of his face.

"No babe, he's dead," Jamal shook his head. "He was only twenty-two years old. Twenty-two years old and strung out on heroin. And the sad part is it didn't have to end for him like that." They were silent for a moment as Jamal's thoughts began to wander. "The detectives told my uncle and aunt that his overdose may have been on purpose."

"You mean on purpose like he committed suicide?"

Jamal shook his head again. "No, I mean like, murdered." He looked at Tiffany and she searched his face.

"Are you serious? Why would anyone want to kill your cousin?"

Jamal shrugged. "I don't know," he mumbled. "I don't know."

"Maybe it was a drug beef. I mean, no disrespect to your cousin, if he was in too deep, it's no telling what he was doing and who he crossed." Jamal thought about what his girlfriend said and then looked at his watch and retrieved his cell phone from his jacket pocket. He made a call over to the station and left the room for privacy. He hadn't told Tiffany about his father's possible involvement in Samir's murder. They had only been dating for four months and though he had fallen for her harder than he anticipated, he knew there were things in his life he could not share with her.

Jamal waited patiently for the phone to be answered. He was just about to give up after the fifth ring when someone picked up.

"Yo Pete, what's going on?" Jamal spoke quietly into his phone.

"Well, considering it's damn near four in the morning, I would think sleep would be going on for those who are fortunate enough not to be in the pit on the late night shift," Pete replied sarcastically. "This ain't nobody but Jamal."

Jamal chuckled. "Listen, I need a huge favor."

"When don't you need a favor, my man?"

"You're right, but this one is important. Are you still cool with that sergeant over at the 8th?"

"Yeah, we still hang out. Why, what's up?" Pete asked.

"I need an update on Samir Muhammad's case. I need any and everything that's on file for his murder investigation. But you can't let anybody know that it's for me." Jamal waited with a hopeful expression.

"I don't know, Jamal. They've been keeping a tight lid on that case, I mean, nobody is talking. Why are you looking into it? Shit, as many problems as that sonuva bitch caused all of these years, especially what he did to you, I'd think you of all people would be glad that the bastard is dead and would keep it moving."

"Pete, can you get the file or not? I'm not looking into this because I want to catch whoever did it. If I could, I'd shake the man's hand who pulled the trigger." Jamal thought of the irony of shaking his father's hand after all of these years and held back a chuckle.

"Then why…?" Pete tried to ask.

"I have a hunch about something. Just please, if you can get whatever information you can about his murder, I'd appreciate it."

Pete sighed and shook his head but knew he could not turn his friend down. "Alright, I'll do it."

Jamal let out a sigh of relief. "Thanks a lot."

"Yeah, don't thank me yet. And no one can know that it's for you. Any reason why?"

Jamal hesitated. "I can't say."

"Uh huh," Pete said suspiciously. An awkward silence followed and Jamal prayed Pete didn't ask him anymore questions. "I could get into a lot of trouble for this."

"I wouldn't ask if it wasn't important," Jamal told him.

Pete sighed. "Alright. Give me a couple of days. I'll see what I can come up with."

"Thanks Pete," Jamal said. They said their goodbyes and then hung up. He took a hold of the ring he still wore around his neck and played with it between his fingers as he leaned on the bathroom sink and sighed. The more he thought about his cousins Braheem and Samir, the more he feared the connection was his father. Out of habit, Jamal kissed the ring and let it fall back against his chest before joining his girlfriend back in their bedroom.

4

The following days were extremely hard for Norman and his wife, Denise. Though there was an outpouring of love and support from their family and Braheem's friends, Norman was feeling uneasy once he received a call from the detective letting him know his son's death was being ruled as a homicide. That wasn't really news to Norman as he had already believed that the moment the detective stated that it was a possibility. The question that constantly stayed with him was why?

Denise was able to get in contact with Braheem's ex-girlfriend and his son's mother, Aminah, to inform her of Braheem's passing. Though Aminah and Braheem had been separated for more than a year due to his dope usage, she always hoped in the back of her mind that he would clean himself up and they could be a family. The fact that it would never happen now and her son would grow up fatherless killed her inside. She decided to let their son

ATR 3: The Wrath of Andre

Brandon, spend some time with "mom-mom" and "pop-pop" in hopes it would bring them some comfort.

Aminah was bringing Brandon to the house for the afternoon. When Norman opened the door to welcome his grandson into his home, Aminah handed him an envelope.

"A man just gave me this and asked me to give it to you," she said to Norman.

Norman opened the envelope and pulled the slip of paper out immediately recognizing the handwriting of his brother, Andre.

"Watch your back in the coming days, Norm. Braheem was killed in retaliation and I don't think it's over. Burn this after you get it."

Norman stared at the paper for a long time. He read the warning from his younger brother again and again as his suspicions were confirmed.

"Is everything okay, Mr. Norm?" Aminah asked after she saw the concerned expression on his face.

"Yeah, everything is fine, sweetheart," Norman mumbled as he folded the piece of paper up. "Did you see which way the guy who gave this to you went?"

Yani

"Umm…" Aminah looked around. "I think he walked up the street. I'm not sure."

Norman nodded his head. "Hey Lil' Man!' he said excitedly as he turned his attention to his grandson. He scooped him up in his arms and hugged him tightly.

"Hi Pop-Pop!" Brandon said with glee.

"I didn't get a chance to get his hair cut because I had a lot of running around to do with the new apartment."

"Oh no, don't worry about it. I'd love to hang with Lil' Man at the barbershop. And then afterwards, we can get some water-ice and pretzels. How's that sound?"

"Awesome!" Brandon said with a huge grin on his face.

Aminah smiled as she rubbed her hand across her son's head before planting a kiss on his cheek. "Thanks so much for keeping him while I work. Daycare has been murder on my pockets since welfare keeps telling me I make too much for subsidy."

"No, thank you. I'm glad you allowed me and Denise to be a part of his life. Whenever you need to bring him over, if you have to work or just need a break, give us a call and bring him on by," Norman told Aminah as he bounced Brandon in his arms.

"Thanks Mr. Norman," Aminah said gratefully. She kissed her son once more and left to run her errands.

Norman sat Brandon down on the couch and turned on *The Backyardigans* for him to watch. He then went into the kitchen. He took the note from his pocket and read it again. He wished he could talk to his brother to get more details on the warning he was giving him. What would make him think that his life is in danger?

He turned the stove on and set the note aflame as his brother instructed him to just as his wife was coming into the kitchen.

"Norman, what on earth are you doing?" Denise asked as she rushed over to him. She made him drop the burning paper in the sink and turned the water on to extinguish the partially burned paper. It hissed and crackled as smoke rose from the sink and the smell of burnt paper filled the air. Denise looked at her husband confused as he took the blackened burned paper from the sink and threw it into the garbage can. "Norman?"

"It's nothing, honey," Norman replied with his back to her.

"Something is going on with you. I don't know what it is but we have enough to deal with, with Braheem's death and his funeral."

"His murder," Norman corrected her.

Denise bit her lip and forced back the tears that threatened to fall. "Baby, I can't do this by myself. I don't know what is bothering you, but I need you to pull it together for me and for our son."

Norman sighed and turned to hug his wife. "I'm here, woman. I just got a lot on my mind. But I'm here. I ain't going anywhere."

Denise buried her face in his chest and took a deep whiff of his cologne. For twenty-nine years, it remained the same; Issey Miyake. The scent was part of what made her fall in love with him and comforted her from the beginning of their relationship until that very day. She felt his hand rub the back of her neck as if to ease her discomfort and exhaled.

"I'm going to take Brandon to the barbershop to get him a haircut. We should be back in the next hour or so. Do you need anything while I'm gone?" Norman asked his wife.

"Nothing that I can think of. But I'll call you if that changes." Denise looked up at her husband as he planted a tender kiss on her forehead.

"I love you, woman," he said in a low voice. He rubbed the back of her neck again before leaving the kitchen. Denise watched him as he scooped their grandson up in his arms. Brandon giggled with glee and Denise became teary-eyed as he was the splitting image of her deceased son. Seeing her husband and their grandson together took her back to the days when Braheem was that age and used to cling to his father's leg. She blinked away the tears and turned the kitchen sink on to rinse the rest of the blackened residue from the burnt paper down the drain. She was curious as to why her husband was burning paper. Denise was about to open the trash can to retrieve the remnants of the paper when her cell phone rang. She hurried into the dining room to get it from the table and saw it was a private number. Normally she didn't answer calls from private numbers but figured it was someone else offering their condolences for Braheem or offering to come by and help with the funeral arrangements so she answered.

"Hello?" she said as she straightened a few knick knacks on her table. There was no answer so she looked at the face of the phone. She put it back to her ear again after turning the volume up. "Hello?" she spoke again. Still there was silence. There was loud static and then the call dropped. Denise looked at the phone wondering who it was and was about to dismiss it when the phone rang again from a private number. This time she answered with an attitude.

"Hello!" She waited a moment to see if anyone would say anything and then she hung up. She couldn't believe someone would play on her phone during her family's time of grief. She shook her head in disgust and was getting ready to head back into the kitchen when her cell phone rang again.

"Stop playing on my phone you insensitive sonuva bitch!" Denise said close to tears.

"Aunt Denise?" Jamal said with hesitation.

"Who is this?" Denise asked.

"It's Jamal…Keyona's son…"

Denise let out a sigh of relief. "I'm sorry, Jamal. Was that you trying to call me a few moments ago?"

"No. Actually I was trying to call Uncle Norm but he wasn't answering his phone so I figured I would try you. How are you holding up?"

"I'm hanging in there. He just left a little while ago with Brandon to take him to get a haircut. He should be back in an hour or so," Denise told her nephew.

"Oh okay. He went to the one up Ogontz and Tulpehocken?"

"Yeah, that's where he always goes."

"I need to talk to him real quick. I was going to stop by the house but I'll meet him at the shop first and then swing around. Do you need me to do anything or pick anything up?" Jamal asked as he tweaked the alarm to his car and climbed inside.

"No baby, but thank you for asking. I'll see you when you come up." Denise said sounding exhausted.

Jamal disconnected the call and made his way over to the barbershop.

5

Norman sat inside of the barbershop talking about sports with some of the barbers while he waited for Brandon's turn to get in the chair. He checked his watch and saw that he needed to add some money to his meter.

"How much longer?" Norman asked one of the barbers.

"As soon as I finish with this guy here, Lil' Man is next," the barber told him.

"Alright, I'll be right back, I'm just going to put some more time on the meter and grab Lil' Man some chips from the store." He took Brandon by the hand and walked out of the shop. He was digging in his pocket for change when he noticed a man leaning on his car with his head down. He shook his head annoyed and went over to him. Just as he was about to tap him on the shoulder and politely ask him to move, the guy turned and stuck a pistol in his stomach. Norman froze in terror. The man displayed a sinister grin.

"If it's money you want, my wallet is in my back pocket. I'll give it to you and you can just let me and my grandson go," Norman said in a low voice trying hard not to alarm his grandson. He held his hand tightly but moved him a step back so he couldn't see what was going on.

"I don't want your money, Norm. Take a ride with me," the man said.

"You're fucking crazy. No way am I getting in the car with you."

"Would you rather I splatter your fucking brains out in the street in front of the boy?"

Norman searched the man's face to see if he was bluffing and quickly saw that he was not. "At least let me take my grandson back in the shop. I'll go wherever you want me to go…"

"Shhh," the man said as he pushed the gun further into Norman's stomach. "He comes, too."

Norman began to breathe heavily, fearing that his life and his grandson's life were in danger. "Please…"

The man was growing impatient and did not want anyone passing by to see what was happening.

He jerked Norman towards his own car. "Shut the fuck up and get in the car."

Norman looked down at his grandson and held his hand tightly. "Change of plans, Brandon. We're going to take a ride with this man here. But as soon as we're done, we'll get your haircut and go get pretzels and water-ice like I promised, okay?" Norman said as he tried to control his voice. He hoped like hell he didn't just lie to his grandson. He prayed even harder that if he didn't make it out of this alive, his grandson did. He reluctantly climbed in the back of the Dodge Magnum and took the ride as instructed.

6

Just as the black Dodge Magnum with Norman, his grandson and the two other men was pulling out of the parking space, Jamal was pulling around the corner.

"Good looking on freeing up the parking space," he mumbled to himself having no idea that his uncle and little cousin were just taken. He parked his car and checked the meter seeing that he had forty-five minutes. He then twirled his keys on his finger and headed into the barbershop.

"Yo Skip!" Jamal spoke to the barber.

"Oh shit, we got the boys in blue in the building. Hide y'all shit!" Skip said jokingly as he stopped the haircut he was doing to give Jamal a handshake and a hug.

Jamal laughed as he hugged his old barber and gave him a pat on the back. "You're real funny."

"How you been? What are you doing around here? I thought you were out Delaware, now?" Skip asked as he resumed the haircut.

Yani

"I've been back for almost two years now," Jamal told him as he looked around. "My uncle didn't get here yet?"

"Oh he stepped out to put some more money in the meter and said he was going to take Lil' Man to get some snacks."

"Oh okay, I can wait." Jamal sat down in the chair and watched the NBA high-lights on ESPN. He chatted with the barbers about sports and the NBA All-Star Break that was approaching. He then looked at his watch after he realized he had been sitting for a while. "Damn, which store did he go to?" Jamal asked.

"I'm guessing the Pizza place a few doors from here or the Chinese store," Skip said to Jamal. "I hope he didn't get tired of waiting and left."

Jamal walked to the doorway and looked up the street to see if he saw his uncle coming. He didn't see him but he did see his car. He went over to it when he saw a PPA lady coming and quickly threw two quarters in the meter. The woman snarled at him and Jamal smiled before flashing his badge. Her snarl quickly dissipated and she moved along in silence. Jamal walked back over to the barbershop.

"Did you see him?" Skip asked.

"No…how long were they gone?" Jamal asked as he pulled his phone out so he could call his uncle.

"Well shit, how long were you here?" Skip asked back.

Jamal looked at the clock on the wall. "Almost thirty-five minutes." He dialed his uncle's cell phone number and waited patiently for him to answer.

"He had just stepped out before you got here. No more than five minutes before you got here because I had just started this guy's head."

Jamal didn't respond. The call to his uncle went to voicemail. "Yo Unc, what's good? I came to the shop to meet up with you and just had to stop PPA from slapping a ticket on Betsy. Call me when you get this." Jamal disconnected the call and looked at his phone. He started to get a bad feeling.

"Is everything okay?" Skip asked.

"He wouldn't have walked far especially if he still had to put money in the meter. He wouldn't have left his car," Jamal said mostly to himself.

"The Detective is at work," Skip teased. He and a few of the guys in the shop chuckled. "I'm sure it's nothing. He probably walked to get Brandon a water-ice."

"I'll be right back." Jamal left the barbershop and walked over to his car. He stood there thinking. *"Where the hell are you, Uncle Norm? This isn't like you at all."* He dialed his aunt from his phone again.

"Hello?" Denise answered.

"Hey Aunt Denise, this is Jamal again. Did Uncle Norm come back to the house?"

"No, he didn't. Why, he isn't at the barbershop?" Jamal hesitated for a moment. "Jamal?"

"Aunt Denise, did anything happen at the house before he left?" Jamal asked.

Denise sat up in the recliner. "No…well yeah but it wasn't anything major. I came into the kitchen as he was burning a piece of paper but he said it was nothing. Jamal, what is going on?" Denise asked starting to feel uneasy.

"Aunt Denise, I'm not trying to alarm you or scare you. But I need you to listen to me and don't ask me any questions until I get there. Lock the doors and go upstairs in your room. Don't answer the door for nobody and don't answer the phone. Does Uncle Norm keep the spare key in the same place?"

"Yes…but Jamal…"

Jamal shushed her. "Aunt Denise, please do what I asked you to do. Give me five minutes and I'll be there. Marco…" Jamal said, hoping his aunt caught on. As children, if he and Shawn stayed at their house and were left alone while Norman and Denise left out, whenever they came back in, Denise shouted "Marco", and Jamal and Shawn were to respond "Polo", to let her know where they were in the house.

"Polo…" Denise replied as her lip trembled. She disconnected the call and then locked both the front and back doors. She also locked the windows and then went inside of the dining room closet. She moved a couple of boxes to the side and put the combination into the wall safe that her husband had installed when Braheem's stealing became evident. Inside was a .44 Smithson Wesson. She pulled it from the safe, locked it back and went up to the bedroom as Jamal instructed. Her eyes became teary as she waited anxiously for Jamal to get to the house.

Jamal went back into the barbershop and pulled Skip to the side. "I need a favor," he whispered.

"Yeah, what's up?" Skip asked speaking softly.

Yani

"Something doesn't feel right. I'm sure you know what happened to Braheem."

"Yeah, Norman told me that he OD'ed on some heroin and the cops are ruling it a homicide."

"Okay, I can't get into details, but I need you to keep an eye on my uncle's car. Keep adding change to the meter and if PPA tries to ticket him, call my phone and let them know that car belongs to a Philly Detective. If my Uncle comes back, tell him to call me so I can kick his ass for having me on alert like this."

Skip nodded his head in agreement and shook Jamal's hand before he left. Jamal jumped into his car and drove to his uncle and aunt's house quickly. Before getting out, he pulled his gun from his holster, took the safety off and chambered a round. He walked to the porch looking around to see if he was being watched. When he felt that the close was clear, he bent over as if he were tying his shoe and lifted one of the flower pots so he could retrieve the spare key. He then unlocked the door and went inside. His heart raced as he locked the door behind him. He walked over to the middle of the stairs. "Marco…" he called out to his aunt.

Denise jumped from her bed and opened the bedroom door. "Polo…" She hurried down to Jamal and gave him a hug. "Jamal, what is going on? What is going on?" she asked almost close to tears.

"I don't know. But something doesn't feel right. He's been gone from the barbershop for almost an hour and said he was going to put money in the meter and take Brandon to get some snacks. From what Skip told me, he left out right before I got there but he didn't put money in his meter. If he was going to go someplace further than up the street…"

Denise interrupted Jamal, "He would've driven." Jamal nodded his head in agreement. "What does this mean?"

"You said Uncle Norm was burning a piece of paper when you came downstairs earlier?" Jamal asked.

Denise started walking to the kitchen, "Yeah it was strange. He threw it in the trashcan afterwards." She reached inside of the trashcan and pulled the partially charred paper. Jamal took it from her and laid it on the side of the sink carefully so he could look at it. The message wasn't entirely burned, but the water smeared part of the ink. He was able to make out part of the message telling his uncle to watch his back and saw part of the word "retaliation". He also saw it was signed by Dre.

"What does that mean?" Denise asked unable to make out as much as Jamal did.

Jamal waited a moment as his thoughts wandered. His uncle had been taken and Brandon was with him. "We need to put out an Amber Alert for Brandon."

"WHAT!?" Denise shrieked. She put her hand to her chest breathing heavy as the tears came. She couldn't believe what was happening. Her son had just died and now her husband and grandson were possibly missing. She plopped down in the chair to compose herself.

"This is Detective Jamal Williams from the 22nd District. I need to put out an Amber Alert for a little boy. His name is Brandon Williams. He's three years old and was last seen…" he put his hand over the mouth piece of the phone. "Aunt Denise, what was Brandon wearing?"

"Um… a dark blue, light blue and white striped long sleeved shirt, uh…some dark blue jeans and tanned boots and a gray hoodie," Denise replied as she trembled.

Jamal repeated it back to the officer taking the report. "He was last seen with Norman Williams on Ogontz and Tulpehocken in the West Oak Lane section of Philadelphia outside of Expressionz Barbershop…No, Norman is not suspected as the kidnapper. He's the grandfather. We think he may possibly be missing as well… No, his car was left at the scene for more than an hour…I can't deal with possibly's and maybe's right now. We have a missing three year old boy, now the longer you wait to issue an Amber Alert for him, the more of a chance you'll find him dead instead of alive…Yes, I'm with the grandmother, Denise Williams, right now at 76th and 20th Street Philly P-A, 19138…Thank you." Jamal disconnected the call and let out a deep sigh. He then looked down at his aunt. "They're sending a unit over. Do you have a picture of Brandon?"

Denise pointed to a mantel where Brandon's most recent Christmas picture was. Jamal picked it up thinking how much he looked like his father, Braheem. His cousin was dead, now his uncle and younger cousin were missing as well. *"Who's retaliating for Samir?"* Jamal thought to himself. He played with the ring that hung around his neck as he thought of any possible connections Samir may have had. He really needed that file from Pete.

Yani

"Aunt Denise, where is Brandon's mom?" Jamal asked as he continued to play with the ring between his fingers.

"I don't know. She said she had some errands to run today but I don't recall her saying what time she would be back." Denise put her hands to her face. "I can't believe this is happening."

Jamal knelt in front of his aunt and put his hands on her shoulders. "Aunt Denise, I promise I will do everything I can to make sure Brandon and Uncle Norm make it home safely. That's my word."

Denise nodded her head as she sniffed and wiped her face. "I just don't understand why my family is being targeted."

"I need to make a phone call, I'll be right back," Jamal said as he stood and made his way over to her front door. He stepped outside and called D-Ball.

D-Ball was on vacation in Miami, Florida with Elizabeth. He wasn't due back in Philly for another three days but if things were about to get as crazy as Jamal suspected they were about to get, he was going to need some serious back-up from his partner.

"Please pick up, please pick up, please pick up…" Jamal mumbled to himself.

"Yo partner! What's good homie?" D-Ball answered. He was sitting on the balcony of his hotel suite looking out at the scenery.

"What's up D-Ball? How's things in M-I-A?" Jamal asked.

"Everything is cool down here. Liz is at the spa right now doing her girly thing. I'm at the hotel chilling. What's going on in Philly?" D-Ball asked as he leaned back in his chair.

Jamal took a deep breath and told D-Ball about his cousin's murder. "I think my uncle and my little cousin Brandon were just taken, too."

"Wait, wait, wait. What the fuck? I leave Philly for a few days and all hell is breaking loose? Why would anybody want to kill your cousin and take your uncle and his grandson?" D-Ball asked.

"It's a long story, but it's connected to Samir."

D-Ball shook his head. "Fucking crazy how that muthafucka can still cause problems from the grave. How is it connected to him?"

"I can't say over the phone. This shit is deep. So deep even I'm having a hard time trying to piece this shit together. All I can tell you is a note was left for my uncle to watch his back with something about a retaliation. I couldn't read the whole thing because he burned it and then wet the paper so some of the message was gone. But if this is retaliation like the note said, it's coming from heat that I'm not familiar with. And if they're coming after my uncle…"

"They could be coming after you too…" D-Ball finished. "I know where you're getting at, say no more. I'ma call Liz and let her know we gotta cut this short and we're on the first thing back to Philly. Did they issue an Amber Alert for your little cousin yet?"

Jamal saw two police cars pull up in front of the house. "The cops just pulled up now. Sorry to cut into your vacation with your lady."

"Nah, it's cool. I'll call you before I get on the plane," D-Ball said as he headed back into the hotel room and put his suit case on the bed.

"Thanks. I gotta go," Jamal replied before disconnecting the call.

"We're looking for a Denise Williams and Detective Jamal Williams," the officer said as he walked onto the porch.

"I'm Detective Williams. Come inside." Jamal opened the door for them and waited for them to enter his aunt's home before coming in behind them and closing and locking the door.

The first officer removed his hat and took a notepad from his pocket. "How are you doing, ma'am?" he spoke politely.

"Not good. My husband and my grandson are missing just two days after my son died of an overdose in our bathroom which the police are now ruling as a homicide. I've lived in this house for twenty-three years and have never even had a verbal dispute with anyone. My husband and I are peaceful, God fearing Christians that would rather help a person instead of harm them. I just don't understand who would want to hurt us," Denise rambled.

"Calm down, ma'am. I understand you are upset, frustrated and afraid. We'll get to the bottom of this and work diligently to bring your husband and your grandson home. Do you have a picture of your grandson?" the officer asked.

Jamal handed him the photo that he retrieved from the mantel. They answered the officers' questions giving a description of what Norman and Brandon were wearing when they left the house as well as a recent photo of Norman. Jamal explained to the officers that he was meeting his uncle at the barber shop on Ogontz and Tulpehocken and was told by Skip that Norman had just left mere minutes before Jamal arrived.

"Skip told me that my uncle said he was going to put money in the meter and get my little cousin some chips and come right back. He never put the change in the meter and he never came back."

The officer jotted down what Jamal said. He then got on his walky-talky and put in the Amber Alert information for Brandon. "What is the name of the barbershop that you're uncle took your little cousin to?"

"Uhh…I believe it is called Expressionz. It's on the corner of Tulpehocken and Ogontz," Jamal told them.

"Okay, we're going to head over there and try to obtain video surveillance from the nearby businesses to see if we can maybe get an idea of which direction Mr. Williams and the little boy may have gone in. And you say he's never done anything like this at all?" the cop asked.

"No," Denise replied. "And Norman never walks too far. If he thinks he's even going to go more than one to two blocks from where ever he is, he drives."

ATR 3: The Wrath of Andre

"We'll question the guys from the barbershop as well to see if maybe they can be of any help," the second officer said.

"If it's okay with you, I'd like to come along," Jamal requested as he played with the ring between his fingers.

"Detective Williams, I understand your desire to help bring your uncle and your cousin home, but because you are family, that puts you too close to the situation not to mention, this is out of your jurisdiction," the first cop explained to him.

"I understand that. But these guys would feel way more inclined to talk to me if they noticed anything funny versus talking to regular cops…no offense."

"None taken," the first cop said with a smirk.

"Aunt Denise, will you be okay here by yourself for a few minutes?" Jamal asked.

"Yeah, just in case we're over reacting and Norman comes home, I want to be here when they get here," Denise replied as she fidgeted.

Jamal leaned over and gave his aunt a kiss on the cheek. He then followed the cops outside and they headed over to the barbershop.

They first went inside of the pizza parlor to request the surveillance tapes. The cashier looked at the police with a strange expression and then asked them to wait a moment while she got her manager.

"Can I help you?" an older Italian man asked as he came to the front of the restaurant. He wiped his flour covered hands in a towel as he looked the police officers over.

"We have a possible kidnapping situation in this area and we are trying to get any possible footage between 11AM-12:30PM to try to get an idea of what may have happened. Is it possible we can get your security tapes from around that time?" the first officer asked.

"They haven't been given to you already?" the manager asked, confused.

"What do you mean?" the second officer asked.

"Well two cops came in here just as you did about an hour ago saying the same thing. I already gave them the tapes," the manager said.

Jamal looked at him with a sinking feeling in the pit of his stomach. "You've gotta be fucking kidding me. Please tell me you got a name or a badge number or something?" Jamal asked as he put his hands to his face in disbelief.

The manager winced. "It was busy, during the lunch hour. I didn't want any trouble and certainly don't like the idea of a kid being kidnapped near my store so I gave them the tapes."

Jamal frowned in anger and shook his head. "Did they say what precinct or district they were from? Did they address themselves as Officer anything?" Jamal asked hastily.

The manager thought really hard as it began to occur to him that he had been duped earlier. "Can't say that I remember what district they said they were from but I think one of them said his name was Officer Albright or…"

The cashier interrupted her manager. "Alvarez. I remember because I wondered why he had a Hispanic name but looked Italian."

Jamal hurried out of the store and the second cop followed behind him. He went over to the Chinese Take-Out restaurant a couple doors down and flashed his badge. Both he and the uniformed officer requested their surveillance footage but came up with the same results. An Officer Alvarez had already confiscated the film.

Yani

"This is definitely a kidnapping and whoever is behind it knows exactly what they are doing," the uniformed officer said.

"What about traffic cameras? Are there any around here on this intersection?" Jamal asked. Panic could be heard in his voice.

The first officer came out and joined them. "Not that I'm aware of but I'll call over to our sergeant to find out."

Jamal walked over to the barbershop but Skip wasn't there. Instead, the other barber Rez was inside. When he saw Jamal, he stopped the haircut that he was giving and went over to him.

"Jamal, what's going on? Two cops just came in here about an hour ago asking if we had any surveillance footage because of a possible kidnapping. Are your uncle and cousin okay?"

"Please tell me you didn't give them shit?" Jamal asked in a low voice.

"Well no, because for one, we don't have video surveillance. But even if we did…I wasn't giving them shit without a warrant."

"Someone took my uncle and my cousin when they left out of here earlier," Jamal said, continuing to speak in a low voice.

ATR 3: The Wrath of Andre

"Get the fuck outta here!" Rez said with his mouth gaping open. "I heard what happened to Braheem. Does this have anything to do with it?"

"I don't know…I don't know. Where's Skip?" Jamal asked. He looked up at the TV and saw the Amber Alert for his cousin scroll across the bottom of the screen. His phone then went off with the Amber Alert as well. This was all surreal to him. He had just finished dealing with Samir and corrupt cops almost two years prior and had hoped that he didn't have to go up against anymore any time soon. He had a funny feeling that it wasn't just corrupt cops behind what was going on.

"He ran over to the bank to make some deposits. He should be back in about an hour. You need me to give him a message?" Rez asked.

"Yeah, tell him to call me when he gets back," Jamal said as he backed out of the barbershop.

"Which car is your uncle's?" the first officer asked.

"The 2001 Chevy Blazer," Jamal said as he pointed to it.

"We're going to need to impound it for evidence. You know the procedure; once we've done whatever search we need to do on the vehicle, your aunt or uncle, if he resurfaces, can come with the proper documentation and pick the vehicle up."

Jamal nodded his head as the officer explained things to him. He looked around, filled with worry over what was transpiring. He wished like hell he could get in contact with his father to find out what the hell was going on. But with his uncle missing, there was no way he could begin to look for him. He began walking away from the officers as they used tools to get inside of Norman's car. Jamal dialed Pete from the police station and waited for him to answer.

"O'Connor," Pete answered after the first couple of rings.

"Hey Pete, this is Jamal."

"Hey my man! How's everything going?"

"Not good…not good. And I can't get into it over the phone. It wouldn't be wise for me to get into it over the phone. Listen, did you get anything on my cousin's heroin overdose or Samir's murder?"

"Actually, I have something on Samir's murder coming over in the next hour. When I say you owe me big for this one, I mean super colossal," Pete chuckled. Jamal was silent as his mind was everywhere and he was having trouble focusing on anything. Pete noticed his silence and cleared his throat. "What's going on?"

"Was any info given to you verbally?" Jamal asked hesitantly.

"Well, Katie said she took a peek at the information she pulled for me and some separate file was with it. Had something to do with an Andre Williams and an Alekzander Kristoff. Funny you two got the same last name, right?" Pete chuckled again.

Jamal was still silent as his heart raced in his chest. "Pete, I gotta go. Call me the minute you get your hands on that file. But whatever you do, don't open it. Don't look through it, read it, nothing," Jamal said hastily.

"What? Why not? Hey, Mally I know you said not to ask any questions but something is up and you got me a little concerned over here. You sure you don't want to tell me what's going on?" Pete asked as he switched the phone from his left ear to his right ear and swirled around to his desk for a little more privacy.

"Trust me Pete, the less you know, the better. I gotta go. Call me when you get the file." He disconnected the call before Pete had a chance to ask him anymore questions and jumped into his car. He sped off and drove back to his aunt's house. When he got there, all hell was breaking loose.

"Where is my son?!" Aminah was practically screaming.

Jamal tweaked the alarm to his car and rushed inside of the house.

"I leave my son alone with y'all for a couple hours and now there's an Amber Alert out for him!! What the hell is going on?! Where the hell is my son??" Aminah was understandably frantic and in tears.

"I'm sorry, Aminah! We're doing everything we can to find him," Denise said in tears.

"Right now you're not doing shit! You're sitting in the got-damn house while my son is out there missing! You're his got-damn grandmother and you can't tell me where the hell my son is?!" Aminah was practically screaming. Jamal grabbed her and hugged her. She held onto his shirt tightly as she cried hysterically.

"We're doing everything we can to find your son and my uncle, trust me when I tell you. We have as many available cops as possible on the lookout for him, alright? We're going to bring him home safely, okay? Just try to stay calm, alright? Just try to stay calm," Jamal said to her softly as he hugged her. He continued to hold her until she started calming down.

"I knew I shouldn't have brought him over here. Whatever Braheem did that got him killed is falling back on my son now. I should have kept him with me. I never should have left him," Aminah said in tears.

"It's not your fault and we don't know if he was kidnapped because of something Braheem may have done," Jamal tried to tell her.

"But you know for sure that he was kidnapped?" Denise asked. Jamal looked at her sorrowfully and nodded his head. Denise put her hands to her mouth and slid into the dining room chair as her legs no longer would support her standing up.

Moments later the local news station knocked on the door to interview Denise and Aminah. Jamal was on camera with them also as they made their plea for Brandon and Norman to be returned home safely. What bothered Jamal is that Norman and Brandon had been missing for more than three hours and a call for a ransom amount had not been made. No form of contact in regards to the kidnapping had been made with them. Typically, that was not a good sign. He prayed like hell that whoever took them wasn't heartless enough to kill Brandon. He rightfully assumed that Norman was taken as a way to get his father to make an appearance. And he feared the torture that they could have been putting his uncle through. Norman told Jamal that he had no idea where Andre was and Jamal knew that even if his uncle did know, he wasn't telling. Jamal knew the chances of his uncle making it back home alive were slim to none. But he prayed little Brandon was spared.

While the news crew was still with Denise and Aminah, Jamal received a call from Pete letting him know the information he was looking for was at the precinct.

"Aunt Denise, I have to make a run to the station for some info that was just dropped off for me in regards to another case that I'm working on. I'll only be gone for maybe an hour or two. But if anything happens, call me. If anybody calls you about Brandon or Uncle Norm, call me first and then call the police," Jamal instructed.

Denise nodded her head before giving her nephew a hug and squeezing him tightly. He grabbed his jacket and left the house. Moments later, the news crew left after him.

ATR 3: The Wrath of Andre

Denise was in the kitchen putting on a pot of coffee. She was extremely exhausted and trying her best to keep it together. She desperately needed Norman there to wrap his arms around her like he always would to make her feel safe. She wanted to bury her face in his chest like she had done for the last twenty-nine years to smell his cologne. She began praying hard that both her husband and her grandson were returned home safely. She was willing to make a deal with the devil himself if need be.

She was just about to turn and leave out of the kitchen when she saw the screen door to her deck open. She froze in terror as she waited for a knock or for Norman to use his key. When neither happened, she hurried to the door and frantically opened it. She was about to blurt out Norman's name but was stopped dead in her tracks as she stared down the barrel of a gun.

"Don't scream. Don't move," the sinister man said in the darkness. Without the light to the deck on, she couldn't see his face but she could clearly see the chrome barrel as if it were broad day light outside. The man reached behind him and produced a frightened Brandon whose eyes and mouth were duck taped. He had earplugs in his ears with music playing to block out the sound around him, keeping him from identifying any of his kidnappers by the way they looked or the way they sounded. Denise opened her mouth and gasped but quickly closed it when the barrel of the gun was pushed closer to her face.

"I said don't talk," the sinister man said in an even more frightening and commanding tone.

With a shaking hand, she reached for her grandson while keeping an eye on the gun. When she felt his shirt, she yanked him over to her and put her arms around him. She then looked around as the sinister man backed away slowly.

"Where's my husband?" Denise asked with her voice trembling. "Where's Norman?"

The sinister man backed slowly down the stairs. "Be glad we brought your grandson back to you," he said coldly.

Denise strained to see the man in the dark. "What does that mean? What do you mean?"

"There's another man with a gun aimed at you. If you so much as move, bend over, sneeze or cry out before I am in the car and pulled out of your drive way, he will kill you and he will kill your grandson, is that understood?" the sinister man asked.

"Yes…yes," Denise stammered.

The sinister man walked the rest of the way down the stairs and got into his car. He pulled out without turning on his lights so she could not see his license plate and turned down the driveway before disappearing into the darkness. Denise waited a few more moments just to be safe and then quickly came into the house, slammed and locked the door.

"Aminah! Aminah, get in here!" she said in tears as she tried to gently pull the duct tape from Brandon's eyes and mouth.

Aminah rushed into the kitchen and hollered out when she saw her son. "Oh my God, Brandon! Baby, are you okay?" she asked as she felt all over him and practically snatched him away from Denise. "Where did he come from?" she asked as she looked at Denise confused.

"A man just came to the back door. He had a gun in my face and told me not to move or say anything. When he gave me Brandon, I asked him where was Norman…" Denise trailed off and burst into tears. "He said I better be glad they brought my grandson back to me," she wailed as she feared for her husband's life.

Aminah held her son who was none the wiser as to what was going on while Denise hurried back into her living room to retrieve her cell phone so she could call Jamal and tell him what happened and then call the police.

7

The basement was dark and damp with one bulb lit in the center of the ceiling casting a dim light throughout a portion of the room. Though the windows were glass brick and partially boarded, a draft managed to get in, meekly blowing around. Norman sat limp in a chair with his hands tied to the back. His face was bruised and bloody after suffering a beating. And though he fought hard, there wasn't much he could do with three against one.

Norman peered up toward the ceiling out of his left eye with the dim light shining down causing him to wince. He looked around for his grandson in a panic when he did not see him and began to jerk his hands at the restraints. He swore to himself that he would do whatever he had to do to get back home to his wife.

The men, led by Alekzander Kristoff, wanted to know where Andre was. They were positive that there was no way Andre was back but didn't make contact with his older brother. They threatened Norman with a promise of coming after Keyona, Jamal, Shawn as well as Shawn's two children if he didn't cooperate. All of that was for nothing because he had no idea where Andre was but he pretended as though Andre was dead as he believed he was for over twenty years. Kristoff didn't believe him. They left him in the room alone for some time giving him one last chance to tell them what they wanted to know with the promise that his death would be quick and painless. Or as Kristoff warned, if Norman kept fucking around, they would kill him slow until he begged to die. Neither was an option for Norman as he vowed he would make it out alive by any means necessary.

Norman jerked at the restraints some more, murmuring under his breath, praying to every God known to man to help him out of this situation. He had been a good man all of his life and just didn't understand if there was a God, why this was happening to him? He jerked once more, feeling the restraints slack a little giving him a tiny bit of wriggle room. He closed his eyes, thanking Jesus, God, Allah, Buddha and every other spiritual entity as a tiny bit of hope that he would survive began to rise in him. Just as he began to think what he could possibly do in the event that he was able to get loose, the door opened and Kristoff along with two other men came inside.

"Ahhh, I see you are awake now. I trust that you are ready to talk?" Kristoff said coolly as he paced pass Norman with his hands in his pockets.

Norman looked at him and his goons but did not respond. He discreetly began to stretch his fingers on a painful angle to begin clawing at the ropes so they would slide down his hands and come off.

"What annoys me about you niggers is that you never take the easy route when it's most important. Oh sure, you want shit to be handed down to you with this belief that this country owes you something," Kristoff said as he paced in front of Norman before leaning against a metal table. "You niggers are just ass backwards. When it's time to work hard, you want to be lazy and have things easy. But here I am giving your black mooly ass an easy option, but you want to take the hard route." Kristoff shook his head with a smirk on his face.

"My brother is dead. He's been dead for more than twenty years. You're wasting your time," Norman said, trying to buy himself some time as he was able to get one of his hands free. He glanced at both of the guys and noticed the door was cracked just a bit. He figured if he could knock at least two of them down, he could make a run for it. He stared back at Kristoff.

Kristoff wagged his fist at him as his face lit up in fury. "You little mother fucker," he said with malice. He reached in his back pocket and pulled out a photo before coming close to him so he could put the photo in Norman's face. "I guess the dead has arisen," Kristoff said.

Norman looked at the photo, recognizing it as one of the pictures that Jamal showed him from Samir's surveillance when they first realized that Andre was very much indeed alive. He stared at the photo for a moment as if it was the first time he saw it and then looked Kristoff in his face.

Kristoff tilted his head up a little to expose his throat. A scar that appeared to be more than six inches in length went neatly across his throat, left to right. A little more up top would have done the job. "Your thug fucking brother is going to pay for this shit. Killing you will just be icing on the fucking…"

Kristoff never got the rest of the words out. Norman hit him with a swift right hook and quickly wrapped the rope around his neck with his left hand.

He head butted him and then grabbed him before shoving him into one of his men. As they fell back, Norman threw himself backwards out of the chair and grabbed it by the legs as he rolled onto his side. He swung it at the second guy who was coming for him and then scurried to his feet to make a run for it. Air pumped in and out of his lungs as his mind raced hoping and praying that he made it. But hope was dashed as Kristoff fired at him, hitting him in his upper left thigh. He yelled out, reflexes causing him to reach for his leg as he staggered, almost falling to the ground. He limped on as his heart raced and Kristoff fired again, hitting him in his right calf. Norman went down. He dragged himself to the door that he almost made it to before Kristoff was standing over top of him. Pissed off that Norman got the drop on him, he kicked him in his back and in his ribs as though he were a dog and then turned him over.

"Sneaky little nigger," Kristoff said as he wiped the blood from the corner of his mouth. He reached in his pants pocket and pulled out a cigar cutter and grabbed Norman's left hand. Norman struggled, having an idea of what Kristoff intended to do, and hollered out in a fearful protest for him to stop. His pleas fell on deaf ears as Kristoff stuck

Norman's ring finger that held his wedding band, through the cigar cutter and proceeded to slicing his finger off. Norman screamed and writhed in pain trying his damned best to pull his finger free but to no avail. The cigar cutter did its work, snatching Norman's finger away in a clean cut.

Norman screamed a high pitched howl, "Muthafucka! I don't know where he is. Fuck you, muthafucka! Kill me if you want to, you spick-ass bitch! What you do to me won't be SHIT compared to what Andre does to you when he gets his fucking hands on you!" Norman yelled as spit flew from his mouth. He took deep breaths against the pain. He knew this was the end for him and he began to silently repent for any offenses he may have made during his time on Earth.

"I'll take your fucking word for it," Kristoff said with the most evil grin Norman had ever seen a man display. His two goons grabbed Norman by his arms and dragged him back to the basement room that he was in and flung him into a chair. His legs felt like they were both on fire and his finger felt even worse. He cradled his hand before the men snatched him up and forced him back in the chair. This time, they tied one of his arms to one of the chair arms and tied his other arm to the other chair arm. He looked up at Kristoff trembling, not out of fear but in pain and anger.

"Take his pants off," Kristoff instructed his men.

They went over to Norman and took his pants and boxers off. Norman kept his eyes on Kristoff as he took slow, deep breaths.

"Where's Andre, Norman?" Kristoff asked, casually.

Norman stared at him and then smiled, "Fuck you, bitch," he said in response.

Kristoff sighed and shook his head. "Like I said, niggers always insist on doing things the hard way…"

They tortured Norman for two hours, burning him with a long grill lighter, putting cigarettes out on his face and hands and even castrated him. But Norman would not budge. He had an idea of where Andre was, but since he was going to die anyway, there was no point in giving up his brother. As much pain as he suffered through, he still refused.

His resilience angered Kristoff, but seeing how much damage Norman was willing to take rather than sell out his only brother made Kristoff respect him just a tad. But he was growing tired of this torture session and decided to end it.

"Where you think you may be protecting your brother, it's going to cost you your nephews and their nigger wench mother. Eventually he'll show his face, even if it's to identify yours."

Norman kept his eyes on Kristoff knowing exactly what was coming next. He watched as Kristoff took out a 9MM. He slammed the clip in which was filled with hollow tip bullets. And like the trained marksman he was, he shot Norman twice in the chest and once in the head quickly killing him.

Kristoff stared at him for a moment before he holstered his gun. "That was one big, tough nigger. Fought his ass off," he said as he continued to stare at Norman's lifeless body. "What a fucking waste."

Norman's body was wrapped in clear plastic, defiling him by stuffing his penis in his mouth. His body was thrown in the back of an old Cutlass 88 and driven to the parking lot of Penndot near 72nd and Ogontz Avenues. His severed finger with his wedding band attached was placed inside of a small gift box along with the wedding ring he received from Braheem as payment for the dope that led to his death, and then wrapped neatly with a bow on it. It

ATR 3: The Wrath of Andre

was then placed in an envelope, addressed to Denise Williams and placed in the mail box.

8

Forty-eight hours had passed by and there was still no word on Norman. Neighbors stopped by offering prayers of comfort for not only Braheem, but for Norman's safe return. They lit candles and held prayer circles to show their support for Denise who at this time, was almost out of her mind with worry. Police kept in steady contact with her and Jamal and they canvased West Oak-lane as well as parts of Germantown and Mt Airy, passing out flyers with Norman's photo in hopes that somebody would be able to give them a lead that would bring Norman home safely.

Though Jamal didn't want to believe it, being a Detective gave him the experience to know that if a missing person had not returned in 24 hours, more than likely, they were dead. He also understood that if a person was taken but no ransom was requested, the intentions were to kill them. He didn't speak of this information to his aunt as he knew that it was important for her to stay positive that her husband and life-time partner would come home safely. Jamal didn't know that after her encounter with the dark and sinister man who returned Brandon to her, she partially understood that she would be burying her husband just as she was planning to bury her son.

Aminah stopped by on the third day that Norman was missing with her son Brandon. She wanted to apologize for how she reacted towards Denise when she found out that her son had gone missing.

"It's okay, sweetheart. I understand. I'm a mother of five so I more than likely would have reacted the same way had it been one of my children who had gone missing under the care of someone else." Denise stepped to the side so she could let Aminah and Brandon in.

"Oh, we can't stay, Mrs. Denise. I just came to let you know that me and Brandon are going to spend some time with my family down in Georgia. I don't mean any harm but I don't feel safe up here and I don't feel like my son is safe either. I don't know what Braheem did to cause himself to get killed and then your husband and my son were kidnapped, but whatever is going on, I'm not trying to have my son in the cross-fire. I got lucky the last time when they returned him. I don't want to take that chance again," Aminah explained.

Denise's heart sank into her stomach. First her son, then her husband went missing and now her grandson was leaving as well. She shook her head in sorrow. "I understand, sweetie. I wish there was something I could say to change your mind, but I understand Brandon's safety comes first." She knelt down and hugged her grandson tight. "You be good for the grandma, you hear? And hopefully I'll get to see you soon."

Brandon nodded his head before Aminah pulled him close to her.

"I'm sorry we won't be here for Brandon's funeral. But honestly, I don't think I would have been able to handle seeing him like that. And I hope everything works out and Mr. Norm is found safe and sound. You all were really good to me and Brandon and helped a lot but…I need to keep my son out of whatever is going on," Aminah said.

Lost for words, Denise nodded her head and hugged Aminah tightly as tears filled her eyes. She rubbed Brandon's head and said, "Call me sometime and let me know if you need anything while you're down in Georgia."

"I will. See you later, Mrs. Denise." Aminah took her son by the hand and left the porch to climb inside of the minivan that was waiting for her. As the van was pulling off, the mailman came onto the porch to hand Denise her mail.

"Good afternoon, Mrs. Williams. How's everything?" the mailman spoke in his usual cheerful manner unaware of everything that was going on.

Denise looked through the regular white envelopes and stopped when she came to the manila envelope that appeared to have a small box inside. "Everything is fine, Melvin. You have a good day," she mumbled as she looked the package over. She went inside of the house and closed the door behind her. After flipping through the other letters and seeing it was mostly junk mail minus a few cards from family out of town sending their condolences and prayers, she came back to the manila envelope. The first thing that she noticed was that there was no return address, which struck her as odd. She shook the envelope only hearing the small box inside briefly shake. She looked at the envelope again and tapped on it with her fingers thinking if she should call Jamal. She finally decided that calling her nephew over a simple package wasn't necessary and began tearing into the envelope to open it. Seeing the bow on the box she began to smile wondering who would send her a gift. She held the box in her hand as she looked inside of the envelope to see if a note or anything had been left. When she saw that there was nothing else inside, she proceeded to open the box.

No amount of logic or reasoning could have prepared Denise for what she was seeing. Her heart raced as it took her brain time to make her understand what she was looking at. Louder and louder her heart beat could be heard in her ears. Her mouth opened to scream once she finally accepted the fact that she was looking at her husband's finger with his wedding band still attached to it. The wedding band that she put on his finger twenty-five years prior to this moment; the wedding band that matched the one taken by her son to pay for the dope that resulted in his demise.

"Jesus!" she yelled as she threw the box on the floor, beginning to hyperventilate. "Oh my God! Oh my God!" she yelled as she struggled to get control of her breathing. She grabbed a hold of the arm rest to her living room chair to keep herself from falling onto the floor as she suddenly felt dizzy and nauseous. It was almost as if she had been placed on a sadistic Ferris wheel and spun around in a speedy manner that was too much for her to handle. She closed her eyes in part to avoid staring at her husbands severed finger and in part to stop seeing the living room spinning in a lop sided and tilted way. She took multiple breaths in an effort to breathe as well as in an effort to keep the contents of her breakfast from flying out of her mouth. Denise let out a gut wrenching yell filled with agony, fear and defeat. Her yell transformed into a high pitched, tearful scream again and again.

A neighbor, who happened to have been trimming her bushes and tidying up her lawn, heard Denise screaming and rushed over to her door. She knocked at first, calling out Denise's name loudly. But when she received no answer and only heard the loud, piteous screams and cries, she twisted the door knob and was grateful that it opened. She went inside and tried her best to calm Denise down but Denise wasn't hearing her. She wasn't hearing anything. Her mind was still focused on her husband's severed finger which was now lying on her floor. Her neighbor, Cindy, grabbed her phone from the table and looked for Jamal's number in her phone book. She was familiar with Jamal and knew his presence had been more frequent due to the murder of Braheem and Norman and Brandon's kidnapping.

"Williams," Jamal answered on his Bluetooth as he drove down the street already on his way to his aunt's house to check on her.

"Jamal, this is Cindy…"

"Wait, I can't hear you… Who is that screaming in the background?" Jamal asked with a frown.

Cindy spoke louder. "Jamal, this is Cindy, your aunt's neighbor. You need to get here now. I don't know what the hell happened but Denise is in here screaming and crying and I can't get her to talk," Cindy said as she stuck a finger in her ear and made her way over to the kitchen so she could hear Jamal and he could hear her.

"Alright…I'm on my way," Jamal replied. He disconnected the call and haul assed to Denise's house.

When he arrived, Denise had calmed down a bit. But the cries were still loud and she still had not been able to vocalize to Cindy what was wrong. The only thing she kept saying was, "My Lord, Jesus why? Dear God!" Jamal damn near had to slap Denise to snap her back to reality so she could tell them what the problem was.

Shaking, Denise stood as she sobbed and walked over to where she dropped the box that contained the gruesome contents someone was heartless enough to send to her. With a shaking hand, she picked it up and handed it to Jamal. Cindy peeped over his shoulder and then gasped, throwing a hand to her mouth.

"Is that…what I think it is?" she asked in horror.

Jamal stared blankly at the box. Of all the sick, demented and fucked up things he had seen while being a police officer, this was a first for him. Had it been a stranger's finger, he may have been able to handle the situation better. But this was his uncle, his only uncle's finger, packaged and gift wrapped and sent to his aunt, posing as a present someone would send to the love of their life.

"You've gotta be fucking kidding me…" Jamal said.

"He's dead…I know he's dead. I know he's dead!" Denise said as she sobbed.

Yani

"You don't know for sure," Cindy said, still trying to remain positive and praying that people weren't actually that cruel.

"We don't assume he's dead until we get a body…" Jamal started to say to his aunt.

"We have his body part! His finger! His fucking finger is in a box! My husband is dead. I know it, I feel it. I felt it a few nights ago almost as if a piece of me had just been taken away. It wasn't bad enough that they took my son! But those bastards stole my husband from me, too!" She sobbed harder and harder. Cindy wrapped her arms around her to comfort her.

Jamal knew she was right. Norman more than likely was dead. His uncle was the closest thing he had to a father growing up outside of the fake older men like Samir who only wanted to groom him for the streets. Norman opened his home to him in an attempt to help save Shawn and Tamera and kept in constant contact with him throughout college and when he first became a police officer to keep him level headed and focused on the bigger picture. The man he loved and respected more than anyone else in this world, outside of his brother and mother, more than likely was dead and Jamal knew that his life would never be the same.

As much as his heart ached and the tears stung his eyes, threatening to fall, Jamal fought hard to keep them back as he contacted the police to have them send someone over. His anger was becoming over whelming as he wished he could get his hands on the bastard who was setting all of this in motion. It was killing him inside to not know who was retaliating with such brutal and relentless force.

Investigators and Detectives filled the house gathering the box along with its contents so they could determine if it was indeed Norman's finger. They questioned Denise and took her statement before leaving after gathering all of the evidence they could obtain.

It was imperative that Jamal find his father. All of this was transpiring because he decided to return from the dead. As happy as he was to finally have Samir out of the way, something that his uncle told him years before came back to him.

"Karma doesn't miss. Eventually you will pay for your sins and he will pay for his. Karma doesn't always fall back on you directly. Sometimes it hits the people around you."

Yani

Jamal shook his head as he began to naturally assume that whoever was retaliating wasn't finished. He could possibly be a target as well as Shawn.

Jamal froze where he was and thought of his mother. "Fuck…" he said to himself as he closed his eyes. He dug in his pocket for his cell phone and dialed his mother's number.

9

Keyona was heading home from work and made a pit-stop at the market. Despite the fact that Norman was missing and his son was dead, she managed to be in an exceptionally good mood. After all of her years of working at Medimmune, she had finally been given the promotion that she deserved. She planned on calling her son and inviting him and his girlfriend over for a celebratory dinner.

There were far too many groceries for her to carry at once. She grabbed as many as she could and took them to her door step. She began humming a tune to herself as she unlocked her doors and picked her bags up to take them inside of the house. It was completely dark, which struck her as odd because she always left at least one lamp on in her living room. She slid her hand across the wall for the light switch to flick on her ceiling lights but nothing happened. She flipped the switch up and down again and then sucked her teeth.

"Got damn it," she mumbled under her breath as she scooped the bags up in her arms and proceeded inside, leaving her front door open. She almost made it to the kitchen when she began to feel like she wasn't alone in her house. Feeling uneasy, she flipped the switch on her kitchen wall but no lights came on.

"What the hell?" she said out loud. Before she had a chance to go inside of her kitchen drawer and pull out a flashlight so she could check the circuit breaker in the basement, a strong hand went over her mouth. She squealed against the hand and struggled to get away from whoever it was. Her heart raced as she became overwhelmed with fear.

"Shhhh!" he whispered in her ear. "Be still, and be quiet. Don't move," he said calmly. He moved his hand from her mouth and pulled her close to him. Keyona partially recognized the voice and her eyes searched wildly in the dark as she breathed heavily. The man holding her used his free arm to aim in the direction she came from knowing that someone had been following her. They both saw a silhouette at the same time and it took everything in Keyona not to scream. Two silenced shots and the person went down. She covered her mouth.

ATR 3: The Wrath of Andre

"Stay here," the man whispered after a moment. He eased away and went into the living room to close and lock her door. He then reached into his pocket and pulled out a device that partially looked like a car's keyless entry remote and pressed a button. Keyona jumped when her kitchen light and living room lamp came on. She trembled as she peered out of the kitchen and saw the man kneeling next to the person he had shot who undoubtedly had been following her. Even though she recognized him, she had to get closer to see for herself; to make sure that her eyes weren't deceiving her.

"Andre…" she said in a matter of fact manner.

Andre looked up at her but didn't respond at first. He checked to see if the person on the floor was still alive. After he confirmed that the victim wasn't, he stood up. Keyona fixed her eyes on Andre unable to believe it. Even though she recognized his handwriting in the note that he sent to her three months ago and prayed so many nights that he would come to her and physically let her know that he was okay, she still couldn't believe her eyes. She balled her hands into fists and put them to her face, shaking her head before marching over to him and swinging.

Yani

"You sonuva bitch!" she cried as she hit him. Andre put his arms up to cover himself against her punches as she swung again and again. "You sonuva bitch! All this time you were alive! All this time!" she cried some more.

Andre managed to grab her wrists and shook her just a bit to calm her down. "Keys, listen to me!" he tried to reason with her.

"You left me and our sons! All this time, I thought you were dead!" Keyona continued to yell as the tears streamed down her face. "You left me!"

"I never meant for it to go down that way, I swear! It was the only way for me to protect you and Jamal and Shawn," Andre tried to explain.

"You don't know what it was like for me to struggle to raise our sons by myself…" Keyona sobbed and collapsed into his arms. "I can't believe you did this to me."

Andre stroked her head as he held her. "I'm sorry," was all that he could think to say.

"Why didn't you take us with you?" she asked with a sniff.

Andre shook his head, "I couldn't. We needed Samir to think I was dead. If you had left too, they would have tracked you and my boys. We had to

96

make it look real. We had to make it look legit. Believe me when I tell you there were so many times I wanted to come back for y'all."

"But you didn't…"

"Because I couldn't," Andre said as he rested his chin on the top of her head. He waited and wished so long for the moment where he could hold Keyona again. He hated the way things went down and felt the betrayal of everyone who played a part in taking him away from his family.

His thoughts were interrupted when he and Keyona heard her door knob moving as if someone were trying to get in. Andre moved Keyona behind him and aimed his gun at the door just as it opened.

Jamal pointed his gun at Andre and Andre pointed his gun at him, neither expecting to see one another.

"WAIT!" Keyona screamed, jumping in between Andre and her son as her heart raced.

Jamal stared at Andre with wide eyes as he continued to point his gun in his father's direction. Though he had already seen from the pictures his mother showed him more than a year ago along with the photos from Samir's surveillance camera, it was like looking in the mirror, only his reflection was an image of his older self. He couldn't believe he was staring his father in the face.

Though he was happy to see his son for the first time in over twenty-five years outside of the times he followed him, Jamal was still a cop and a possible threat. His expression remained cold and emotionless. "Drop the gun, Jamal," Andre said in a low voice.

"Don't do this you two!" Ms. Keyona said as she looked from her son to Andre. She knew how defiant the both of them were and how they rarely took orders from anyone. The irony that they both had issues with authority yet Jamal ended up becoming a cop danced around briefly in Keyona's mind as she looked from Jamal to Andre. "Both of you put your guns away!" Keyona said with base in her voice. Jamal glanced at his mother who looked terrified to see her son and his father with guns aimed at each other in her house. He could tell by looking at his father that he had no intentions of putting his gun down and he wasn't sure if he wanted to call his bluff. He was about to holster his gun when he saw a man emerge in his mother's kitchen. The person had his gun aimed at Keyona. Jamal fired two shots, putting him down but not before the armed man was able to get one shot off, hitting Keyona in the back and causing her to scream. She fell into Andre and then onto the floor.

"Keyona!" Andre yelled. Before he had a chance to see about the mother of his children, another man was coming through the front with two more coming through the back. Andre threw himself behind a long bench that separated the living room and dining room, and fell into the China cabinet causing it to rock and spill a few items. Glasses crashed to the floor and shattered. He aimed underneath the bench and shot the gunman in his ankle causing him to fall to the floor. Andre then shot him in the head. Jamal was crouched down and fired at the men in the kitchen before diving behind stairs. Andre unloaded his clip into the men coming out of the kitchen also, putting them down. He lay on his back so he could see under the dining room table as well as the bench in case anyone else was coming and pulled a second gun from his waist. He aimed at the back door while aiming at the front door with his other gun, anticipating more company. When all was quiet, he got up and looked down at his son.

"Check her!" he yelled to him as he dumped one clip and slammed another in.

Jamal scrambled to his mother with tears in his eyes. *"Not again!"* he thought to himself as his heart raced and his body shook. He tentatively reached for his mother's neck to feel for a pulse. "Mom," he said in a cracked voice. When he felt a pulse, he laid his head against hers and cried.

"I've gotta go, Jamal. The cops will be here soon. I can't stay," Andre said as he crouched in front of his son.

"All of this is because of you," Jamal said after a moment. He looked at his father with hate in his eyes. "They're coming after us because of you."

Andre searched his son's face knowing that he was right. "Are you arresting me, Detective?" he asked coldly.

Jamal stared at his father. Legally, he had a duty to his badge to turn his father in. But something in his heart wouldn't allow him to commit that kind of betrayal. Instead, he pulled his shirt over his head and applied it to the gunshot wound to his mother's back. He then grabbed his cell-phone and called it in.

Andre began making his way over to the back door.

ATR 3: The Wrath of Andre

"Dad!" Jamal hollered out. Andre looked back at him. "How do I make contact with you? Uncle Norm…"

"Norm is dead," Andre said coldly as he interrupted him. "You know that better than I do. If they haven't found him yet, he's dead. They're watching you. And they'll be listening; the cops and Kristoff. No phone call you make will be private. I know where to find you."

"Kristoff… he's dead," Jamal said, confused.

"Yeah…"Andre smirked. "So was I, remember?" And with those words, he disappeared out of the back door and into the dark night.

"Hold on, mom," Jamal murmured. His head was spinning as he couldn't believe all of this was transpiring. His father said he was being watched. Kristoff was alive and more than likely, his uncle Norm was dead.

Moments later, cops were storming the place. Jamal got out the way while paramedics helped his mother. He looked on the floor and saw the empty clip his father dropped when he re-loaded his gun. While the officers weren't looking, he knelt down as if he were tying his shoe and grabbed the clip. He discreetly stuck it in his pocket just as D-Ball was coming through the door after Keyona was wheeled out and taken away in an ambulance.

"Jamal, what the fuck is going on?" D-Ball asked as Jamal sat in a dining room chair with his hands to his face. "Your mom was shot?"

Jamal nodded his head unable to speak. He refused to cry as hard as it was to hold his tears in. He was confused about so much and was trying to process everything.

"Who would come after your mom?" D-Ball asked.

Jamal looked up at his partner. The look that he gave D-Ball told him enough to let him know this wasn't a conversation to be had in front of so many cops. And after what his father said about him being watched by cops and Kristoff and seeing how cops were obviously involved with his uncle being taken, he wasn't sure of how much he should say and to whom it should be said. He didn't want to assume D-Ball wasn't one to be trusted, but at this time, he wasn't sure of whom he could trust. He did know one thing; Kristoff was alive and was proving to be one of the most ruthless bastards Jamal had ever gone up against.

ATR 3: The Wrath of Andre

"Jamal?" D-Ball asked. Jamal shook his head and looked up at him as though he had been snapped out of his thoughts. "Do you want a ride to the hospital so you can be with your mom?"

"I need to call Shawn first. Can I use your phone?" Jamal asked his partner remembering his father's warning.

D-Ball reached into his pocket and handed Jamal his phone without question. Jamal then went out to his car and sat inside.

It took him a moment to gather up the courage to call his younger brother. More importantly, how was he going to deliver some bad news like that and convince Shawn not come back to Philly when he would more than likely want to be by their mother's side? He started not to tell him, but he knew once Deisha found out, she would tell Chanda and Chanda would tell Shawn and he wouldn't get the chance to convince Shawn to stay in Italy. He was positive that they would be targets and he wanted to keep Shawn and his family out of harm's reach.

Jamal took a deep breath and dialed his brother's number, partially hoping that Shawn didn't answer. Hope was dashed after the third ring.

"Hello?" Shawn answered, not recognizing the number.

"Shawn, it's me," Jamal replied as he watched the cops question the neighbors.

"What's up, Jamal? You got a new number or something?" Shawn asked.

"I wasn't expecting you to be up so late," Jamal said as he looked at his watch and saw that it was after 6pm where he was so he knew it had to be after midnight over in Italy.

"Oh, me and Chanda just came back from an engagement party some friends threw for us. She got me in here looking at wedding shit on-line. This girl about to drive me crazy," Shawn chuckled as he kissed Chanda on the cheek after she licked her tongue at him. Shawn noticed Jamal's silence. He knew from past experiences that if Jamal was calling at an hour when he knew it was super late in Italy, something had to have been wrong. "So…what's up?" he asked.

Jamal took a deep breath. "Shawn, ever since we were kids, I tried to look out for you. I tried to look out for us. A lot of times you didn't listen to me when I told you not to do things. Sometimes we were lucky enough to come out of shit intact but…"

ATR 3: The Wrath of Andre

"Jamal, what the hell is going on?" Shawn asked becoming nervous over his older brother's rambling.

"It's a lot going on, too much for me to explain. I have a lot of shit to tell you and I don't even know where to start," Jamal let out a shaky breath as he thought of their mother.

"Jamal, what the hell is up? You're calling me in the middle of the night rambling about shit. What's up?" Shawn asked again. Chanda looked at him with concern.

"When Samir was killed, I put in a request to have the information from his murder investigation sent to me," Jamal started.

"Yeah…and?" Shawn asked wondering why Jamal would be bringing Samir up and why he would bother looking into his murder.

"They sent me some pictures from his surveillance. I know who killed him."

"Good, send him a thank you card and a bottle of Ciroc. I'm confused, Jamal. Who the fuck cares about who Samir's murderer was…"

Jamal interrupted him, "It was our father, Shawn," he blurted out. There was a deafening silence on the phone that reminded both Shawn and Jamal of the moment in his bedroom many years ago when Jamal told him that Samir had killed their father.

"Braheem is dead," Jamal continued as his voice began to crack. "Someone gave him supped up heroin and he OD'ed in Uncle Norm and Aunt Denise's bathroom right in front of them. Then a few days later, Uncle Norm and Braheem's son Brandon were kidnapped. They brought Brandon back but there's still no word on Uncle Norm, no request for a ransom, no contact or nothing," Jamal continued.

"Wait a minute…what the hell?" Shawn interrupted Jamal as his heart raced and his mind wandered in confusion trying to process everything Jamal was telling him. "What the hell are you saying; that our father is alive? That he's been alive all these fucking years?"

"Shawn, I came to mommy's house today and he was here. Dad was here. I saw him myself…" Jamal trailed off and Shawn was positive he heard Jamal crying. He hadn't heard his brother cry since Tamera was killed. "Mom's been shot."

Shawn stood straight up. "No Jamal. By who?!" he asked angrily. Chanda stood up with him trying to find out what was going on. "I'm coming home," he said.

ATR 3: The Wrath of Andre

"No Shawn, that's why I'm calling you,"

"No? No?! Are you muthafucking serious? All hell is breaking loose at home. You're telling me our dad is back from the dead, he probably killed Samir and because of it Braheem is dead, Uncle Norm is missing and probably dead too and somebody shot mom!? And you expect me to do what? Just sit the fuck here with my thumbs up my ass? Fuck that, I'm coming home!"

"Babe, what's happening?" Chanda asked as her heart raced.

"Shawn, LISTEN TO ME!" Jamal yelled, stopping Shawn dead in his tracks. He had never yelled at Shawn before but the desperation in his voice got his brother's attention. "This ain't like when we went up against Samir and you saved me in the woods, or the time we got jumped and you got shot. This shit is real. At least with Samir, we knew who and what we were up against. But this time we don't. They're coming after any and everybody who's connected to dad and that includes you, and Chanda and y'all kids. I promise you, if you come back to Philly, I'ma personally fuck you up!"

Silence followed Jamal's warning as Shawn didn't know what to say. He wanted to be with his mom. How could he not be by her side after she had been shot? He looked at Chanda and then thought of their children. Even though Jamal was telling him that their father was alive, he knew the pain of growing up without one and did not want his children or Chanda to bear that cross. He closed his eyes and sighed.

"What about mom?" Shawn asked.

"I got eyes on mommy, don't worry. But I got a bad feeling about this one. You know I don't scare easily. But this shit…" Jamal trailed off again as he looked at one of the neighbors talking to a couple of the cops. He saw him point towards the roof tops and had a funny feeling he may have witnessed Andre when he left out the back. "Shawn, I've gotta go. If anything happens, I'll let you know. If you don't hear from me, you'll hear from D-Ball. This is D-Ball's number, so save it to your contacts. I've gotta go." Jamal hung up abruptly when he saw the cop motion for him to come to him. He got out of the car and walked over to him to see what he wanted.

Shawn hung up the phone and looked at it. His mother had been shot. His father was alive and his brother was caught in the middle of some kind of retaliation that already claimed his cousin and possibly his uncle. Chanda put her arms around him and held him tightly. Normally, Shawn would not have hesitated to go back to Philly to back his brother up. This time, he decided against it. Whatever was going on struck fear in Jamal and that was a rarity. He prayed for his brother's safety and his mother's recovery but decided for once in his life to take heed to Jamal's warning and stay home with his fiancée and their children.

10

Jamal wiped his face and stuck D-Ball's phone in his back pocket. This was turning out to be one hell of a week that he was nowhere near prepared for and he had a sneaky suspicion that things were definitely going to get worse.

"Detective Williams," the officer greeted him with a hand shake. "I want to personally offer my sympathies in regards to everything that has been going on with your family this week. We have a witness here that says he saw someone leave out the back of your mother's house and used the ledge out back to climb up to the roof. Did you happen to see anyone else during the shooting? Maybe you scared him away or something?" the officer asked.

Jamal's heart was racing and there was a ringing in his ears. He looked at the witness and then looked up towards the roof tops as he tried to quickly think of a response. He cleared his throat. "I was only aware of the ones who came in the house. If there was someone else, I don't know, maybe I did scare him off. But I didn't see anyone leave out the back. Any chance we can get helicopters out here to canvas the area? He couldn't have gotten far," Jamal asked with a straight face. He knew by now, his father was long gone but he didn't want to send up any red flags.

The Officer turned to the witness, "How long ago was it that you saw this person climb to the roof top?"

"Maybe five minutes before y'all got here. But it's been like almost an hour now, that nigga's long gone probably," the witness assumed.

"So he was Black?" the officer asked as he opened his note pad to write down more information.

"Yeah, I mean I didn't see his face but I could tell by the way his hair was cut and I saw a little bit of his skin complexion that he's definitely Black," the witness described.

"What about height, weight, what he was wearing? I know it was dark, but any details you can give us would help," Jamal asked.

The witness thought for a moment and then shook his head. "If I had to guess I would say he was about your height Jamal, but a little heavier. He wasn't fat but he was built. He had on a leather jacket, uh, some dark pants, not sure if they were jeans or maybe those Dickie pants that guys wear; dark sneakers and a close haircut. I know that's not much to go on. I wish there was more I could give. I knew Ms. Keyona since I was a youngin. She really changed this block with how she started decorating and cleaning up to make it look more cheerful and everybody else just kinda followed her lead. I hope your mom is okay. She's good peoples," the witness said sympathetically.

Jamal placed his hand on the neighbor's shoulder and thanked him before going back inside of his mother's house.

Shattered glass adorned the dining room floor along with knocked over chairs and knick-knacks. Bullet casing had been circled and collected. The holes in his mother's couch pillows and living room walls from the brief shoot out burned in Jamal's mind's eye like digital film, embedding within his memory. He closed his eyes as he thought of his father.

"Where are you, you sonuva bitch?" he mumbled under his breath.

"Where's who?" D-Ball asked, over hearing his partner.

ATR 3: The Wrath of Andre

Jamal looked at him startled, not realizing anyone was in the house. "Nothing, just thinking out loud."

"Yo Jamal, don't be like that. We knew each other too long and done been through too much shit for you to be acting like you can't come to me when it's heat. Regardless the fact that we're cops, you're still my fucking mans, feel me? This shit that went down tonight was outta fucking pocket. Tell me what's going on. You know how I gets down. If a muthafucka wants heat, I'll bring the shit to his door. Anybody that comes after my family, and you, your mom and Shawn has been more of a family to me than my own; they can fucking get it, nigga or bitch. I don't discriminate when it comes to my family," D-Ball said firmly to his friend and partner.

"I appreciate that Dante, but this ain't shit like what we went up against before," Jamal said in a low voice so the cops outside could not hear him. "These niggas came through the front and the back of my mom house. I don't know if they planned to take her like they did my uncle but started blasting because they saw us," Jamal slipped as he began to replay everything over in his mind.

"Us who?" D-Ball asked. Jamal looked at him and didn't respond. D-Ball caught on quickly. "He was here?" he whispered.

"Yeah, that nigga was here, and I'ma tell you, if it wasn't for him, my ass would probably be dead right now right along with my mom.

"You know it's some kind of pull with the cops again. How the fuck else were they able to get the surveillance tapes before I got there when my uncle and cousin were kidnapped? And they knew right when to get those shits too when it would be too busy for anybody to really pay attention to what they looked like or remember their names or question why they needed the tapes."

"What exactly did your father say to you?" D-Ball asked.

Jamal shook his head and spoke in an even lower tone. "The bol Kristoff that you thought was dead, he's alive; very alive. That's who more than likely took my uncle and killed Braheem."

"And more than likely, he's coming after your ass next. What the fuck is up with niggas coming back from the dead and shit? Is this not real life or what? Why can't the good niggas like Kiree and T-Mac come back? Why the fuck is God sending his goons back?" D-Ball asked in a half joking manner.

"Shit, I said the same thing. If y'all niggas think I was ruthless in these streets, trust me, you don't want to go up against Andre…"

D-Ball shushed Jamal when he saw a couple of cops approaching them.

"Detective Williams, Detective Smith," one of the officers greeted them. Jamal and D-Ball nodded at the officers. "What the hell happened here?"

Jamal took a deep breath already having his version of the events ready to tell. "I came to my mother's house to update her on what was going on with my uncle's kidnapping. We were standing in the dining room talking when I saw someone in her kitchen. I saw that he had a gun pointed at my mom, so I pulled my gun and ordered him to drop his. When he didn't, I shot him. Unfortunately, he got a shot off and it hit my mom in the back. I heard another gunman coming through the front and I shielded myself behind her bench. I was able to put down the gunman that came through the front and the two who came through the back," Jamal lied. He had no intentions of giving his father up. He just wasn't built that way. And knowing that there were still dirty cops on the force probably working for Kristoff, he didn't want to risk turning his father in, only for his father to be turned over to Kristoff and killed.

The cops looked at Jamal and then looked at each other. "You have a Beretta, correct?" one of the officers added.

"Yeah, my service pistol."

"The guys on the floor all had 9MM. But a couple of the shells we found on the floor were from a .44 semi-automatic handgun," the officer said suspiciously.

Jamal was stuck for a moment so D-Ball jumped in. "Jamal, didn't a witness outside say he saw a man leave out of your mom's back door?"

Jamal looked at D-Ball wide-eyed. "What?" He was almost in a panic thinking D-Ball was going to implement his father's role in the shooting.

D-Ball sensed Jamal's panic and began to over talk him. "A witness outside said an unidentified man was seen leaving out the back of the residence where he used the ledge out back, climbed onto the rooftop and disappeared. We think it's possible there was another gunman after Jamal and his mom but wasn't expecting the response that was given and more than likely fled the scene. It's possible he may have gotten off a few lucky shots before he ran off," D-Ball looked at Jamal to reassure him that he had his back.

The officers looked at each other again as if they did not believe D-Ball's story. "Okay, we're going to head over to the station and try to piece this thing together. Is there anything you want to tell us to help us understand why your family is being targeted?"

Jamal took a deep breath. "I don't know."

"Seems like it started with your cousin, Samir. And with all of the shit that he was into and all of the lives he destroyed, it's possible that someone is retaliating against him and everyone he is close to," one of the cops assumed.

"No, that's too simple. How do we know this isn't a retaliation because he was killed?" the second cop said. He stared at Jamal to see how he would respond but Jamal was used to holding a poker face and didn't give them any hints as to whether he believed either of their theories.

"Whatever the reason is, my main concern is finding out who's behind it and stopping them before any more of my family gets hurt," Jamal said instead.

"Where is your brother? Is he still overseas?" one of the cops asked.

D-Ball interrupted Jamal before he had a chance to answer, "Hey Jamal, we need to get to the hospital to see your mom. If y'all come up with anything, call us." D-Ball and Jamal headed out of Keyona's house. "We're taking my car."

"How come you didn't let me answer Gomez's question?" Jamal asked as he hopped inside of D-Ball's new 2013 Cadillac CTS.

D-Ball started his car and sped off. "Because why the fuck do they need to know where Shawn is? And how would they know this is retaliation behind something Samir did unless they either know more than we know…?"

"Or are on the other side," Jamal said in a low voice. He took out D-Ball's phone and called his friend Pete.

"Hello?" Pete answered after the second ring.

"Pete, this is Jamal."

Pete looked at his phone not recognizing the number. "Hey Mally, what's up with the new digits? I almost didn't answer."

Jamal hesitated, "My phone died so I'm using my partner's. I need a favor."

"As usual," Pete mocked. "I heard what happened at your mother's house. I've been trying to call you to make sure you were okay."

"I'm fine. Pete, did anyone see the file that you got for me?" Jamal asked hastily.

"I don't know. Katie had it sent over by one of the uniforms. I'm not all sure whose hands or how many hands touched the file before it got to me. Mally, what's going on?"

Jamal shook his head. He hadn't had a chance to look at the file with everything that was going on with his family. But the fact that his father was mentioned in it along with Kristoff and the information may have gotten into the wrong hands didn't sit well with him. "Pete, how much of the file did you read?"

"Not much. I told you that I glanced at it and saw that a suspect by the name of Andre Williams was listed along with a connection to…"

"Wait, he's listed as a suspect?" Jamal interrupted Pete.

"…Yeah. Wait, you haven't read the file yet?" Pete asked, confused.

"No. I've gotta go." Jamal hung the phone up before Pete could say anything else. He then called

Temple University Hospital. "Yes, this is Detective Jamal Williams from the 22nd District. My mother, Keyona Williams, was brought in an hour ago with a GSW to the back. I need information on her condition." Jamal waited patiently for details on his mother to be given to him. The operator advised him that she was still in surgery. "Okay, it's very important that this gets done. When she comes out of surgery and is placed in her room, I need security outside of her door. Nobody, and I mean nobody, gets past to see her unless it is me. Cops are not to come question her, she is not to have any visitors outside of me, her son, Detective Jamal Williams, is that understood?" Jamal gave the operator his badge number and then hung up after being reassured his instructions would be carried out.

"I get the feeling whatever Pete told you wasn't good," D-Ball said as he continued to drive.

"Whatever is in that file is being kept too hush-hush. I need to get home so I can read through it and find out what the hell is going on. This isn't just about Samir. I think this has more to do with my dad than anything else." Jamal's cell-phone went off. He answered tentatively. "Williams."

ATR 3: The Wrath of Andre

"Detective Williams, this is Officer Marley from the 14th District. We need you over at 71st and Ogontz Avenue as soon as possible."

Jamal's heart raced, "Is this about my uncle?" he asked.

"I can't say over the phone. Just please get to the location at your earliest convenience. The parking lot where Penndot and Little Ceaser's Pizza Restaurant is located."

Jamal was quiet for a moment. In his gut, he had a bad feeling that his uncle had been found. "We'll be there as soon as possible." He disconnected the call.

"What's the problem?" D-Ball asked.

"I think they just found my uncle…"

11

At the time Denise was discovering her husband's severed finger inside of a gift box, an even more gruesome discovery was being made mere blocks from her home…

A man walking his Great Dane decided to make a stop at Murray's located in the mini plaza on 71st and Ogontz Avenues. He tied the slobbering hound up to a pole not too far from a dingy, off white colored Old Cutlass 88 and gave the pooch a pat on the head before going inside of the mini market to purchase his lottery tickets and snacks. The Great Dane turned its attention to the automobile and began sniffing. He barked, whimpered and whined as he tried to get close to the car but was restrained by his leash. People walking by looked at the dog but paid it no mind as he seemed hell bent on getting over to the car.

His owner hurried out of the store in fear that someone would try to steal his furry best friend.

ATR 3: The Wrath of Andre

"What's the matter, Brody? What's the matter boy? You don't like being tied up out here?" the owner asked his dog as he rubbed his head. The dog continued to whimper and whine with partial growls in between as he scratched and pawed in the direction of the car. The man untied his dog and Brody immediately scrambled towards the car. It sniffed profusely around the trunk, barking repeatedly. The owner was dumbfounded and had no clue as to why the car was of particular interest to his dog. He went over to it and bent down to grab the dog by the leash so he could lead it in the direction of their home and covered his mouth against the stench that was coming from it.

"What in the hell…?" the owner said with his mouth covered as he coughed and gagged. He noticed a few flies flying around the trunk and then saw what looked like dried blood. He took a couple of steps back as he began to understand why his dog was going crazy about the car.

The owner reached in his pocket for his cell phone and called the police. He explained what he saw on the trunk of the car and the location along with the smell and the reaction his dog was having to the automobile. Though he already planned to do so, the operator asked him to stay where he was and advised him that a unit was being dispatched. The owner disconnected the call and nervously lit a cigarette.

About fifteen minutes later, two police cars were pulling up. The owner, whose name was Charles, had smoked about three cigarettes nervously as he awaited their arrival. He put his last cigarette out and shook the officer's hand after going over to them.

"My dog just started going crazy when I went into Murray's to grab a few things. When I came out to see what the problem was and took him off of his leash so we could head home, he took off to the car and started sniffing, scratching and barking at the trunk. The smell coming from the trunk…I'm hoping not but, I think it's a body in there," Charles said nervously.

"Why would you think that, sir?" the officer asked as Charles showed him to the car he was talking about.

"Well shit, it stinks like a dead body, number one. And number two, look," Charles said as he pointed to the blood stains under the trunk's hood. He covered his nose and mouth as he knelt down to point to exactly where the stains were.

The officer frowned at the stench as well and waved his hand over his mouth. "You might be on to something." He flagged his partner over to him so he could see what was being shown to him. They both observed and then called for back-up.

The officer went over to their squad car and took out what resembled a crow bar.

"Maybe you ought to stand back," one of the officers suggested to Charles. Charles took a few steps back but still peered at the trunk, his curiosity over ruling his common sense.

The officer used his tool to pop the trunk, which gave way with little to no effort. It only opened a quarter of the way but the smell that escaped was even stronger than what they previously smelled. The officer that was closest choked against the stench and fanned his hand in front of his face. Though he couldn't see yet, he was positive that Charles was correct and there was a body inside of the trunk. He tentatively used his foot to lift the hood higher, not wanting to use his hand or lean too close to the trunk. Inside, wrapped in plastic, stinking of death and covered in semi-dry blood was Norman's body.

"Holy shit!" the officer exclaimed. Bystanders who could sense that something wasn't right began to come closer to try to get a better look. Charles too came closer for a better look and almost vomited from the stench and the site. He grabbed his dog and pulled Brody away.

"Clear this area, rope this block off and call it in," the officer who opened the trunk said to his partner.

Other officers came onto the scene along with a rescue wagon, fire truck and a coroner. 71st and Ogontz to 72nd and Ogontz was roped off against civilians to avoid the crime scene being tampered with. The medical examiner on the scene carefully unwrapped Norman's body so he could be placed into a body bag and carried off to the morgue.

"Jesus, whoever did this tortured the hell out of this man. Look at the burn marks on his face and hands," she said.

"Wait, it's a man?" one of the officers asked.

The Medical Examiner looked at him sideways. "This really ain't the time for damn jokes."

"Hey, this day and age, you can't tell who's male and who's female," the officer said with a straight face.

The Medical Examiner shook her head and rolled her eyes. "As I was saying, they burned his face and hands with cigarettes and cut off his genitalia." She lifted his left hand. "They cut his ring finger off as well."

Another officer over heard what was said and went over to her. "Wait, you said they cut his finger off? His ring finger?" she asked.

The Medical Examiner turned to her, "Yes, why?"

The officer looked at the body and closed her eyes. "Sonuva bitch, that's Norman Williams; Detective Williams' uncle. Both he and his grandson were taken last week. The grandson was returned but earlier today, his wife received a package with a severed finger inside. It was taken in as evidence to confirm the identity." She looked at him and shook her head in sorrow.

"Are you sure it's him. Did you see a picture?" another officer asked.

"Yeah, I was helping with the search when it first started. I was really hoping that we found him alive. For some reason, this family is getting hit…literally." She blinked back the tears that threatened to fall before reaching in her pocket and calling Jamal. After hanging up with him she looked down at Norman again sorrowfully. "He's on his way."

12

D-Ball hauled ass over to 72nd and Ogontz. He stopped the car on Walnut Lane and Ogontz and Jamal jumped from the car before D-Ball could fully put it in park. A cop tried to stop him from crossing the line but Jamal pushed him away and kept going.

"He's a Detective!" D-Ball yelled at the officer when he saw him reach for his service pistol. D-Ball flashed his badge and ran after Jamal.

"Wait a minute Jamal," another cop who was familiar with the case said as he grabbed onto him.

"Get the fuck off me, Rob!" Jamal yelled as he tried to yank away.

"I can't let you go over there, Jamal!" Rob said back as he tried to hold Jamal back.

"Rob, that's my fucking uncle! Get off of me! Get the fuck off of me!"

ATR 3: The Wrath of Andre

"Let 'em go, Rob!" D-Ball said trying to separate the two of them. "He needs to identify the body. Let him go," D-Ball said with a menacing look. Rob let Jamal go and Jamal took off running towards the body bag he saw when Rob first grabbed him. His heart raced as he feared the worst. D-Ball was right behind him. Another cop tried to stop him but backed off when he realized it was Jamal. Out of breath and with shaking hands, he reached for the zipper on the body bag and started to unzip it. Since the ordeal began, he did his best to keep his composure but seeing his uncle and confirming that he was dead, seeing the bullet hole in his head and the burns in his face broke through every ounce of his self-control and his face contorted before his eyes teared up. D-Ball shook his head as he placed a hand on Jamal's shoulder and squeezed.

"Is it him?" another officer asked.

Unable to speak, Jamal took a trembling breath and nodded his head. He stared down at his uncle for a moment as the tears fell and shook his head. "I'm sorry, Unc…" he said softly in a shaky voice. He zipped the body bag back up with a shaky hand but still stood over him.

"Tell me what you need me to do and it's done," D-Ball said in Jamal's ear. "Just say the word and I got you. Whoever did this, we will get those muthafuckas, I promise you." D-Ball could feel Jamal's pain as he understood how close Jamal was to Norman and knew how even more closely they had become after Tamera was killed.

Jamal stared blankly as the body bag was placed in the back of the coroner's truck. "Take me to my aunt's house," Jamal said in a shaky voice.

D-Ball nodded his head and waited for Jamal to head back to his car. Officers stopped him to offer their condolences. Jamal barely heard them. He was trying his best to come to grips with the fact that his uncle was dead. It didn't sound right in his head when he thought of it and he didn't even want to imagine how it would sound when he vocalized it to his aunt. The news that he had to share with her was already leaving a bad taste in his mouth and making him sick to his stomach. His aunt was like a second mom to him and Norman was the only father that he knew. He was positive that whoever was striking against his family would strike at him next. Not only did he have to inform his aunt of her husband's murder, but he needed to be on his job ten times more than before to make sure he wasn't caught slipping.

He climbed in D-Ball's car and stared blankly out of the window as D-Ball drove. The closer they got to Denise's house, the harder it was for Jamal to hold his tears in. As fast as they fell, he wiped them away not wanting to share his grief in front of D-Ball.

When they pulled up to the front of Denise's house, Jamal looked at her door but couldn't bring himself to get out of the car.

"You want me to do this for you?" D-Ball offered.

"No, she needs to hear it from me. She'll never forgive me if someone else comes to tell her." Jamal wiped his face and climbed from D-Ball's car. Even though he had a key to his aunt's house, he opted to ring the doorbell. When Denise opened the door, Jamal couldn't meet her gaze. He lowered his eyes and looked at the ground instead.

"Jamal?" Denise asked as she searched her nephew's face. Jamal shook his head still unable to look at her. He opened his mouth to speak but couldn't find the words. Denise saw the tears falling from Jamal's eyes and she put her hands to her mouth. "Norman… he's dead."

Yani

Jamal nodded but still couldn't look at her.
"Yes, Auntie. They found him." Denise shook her
head as she cried. Jamal put his arms around her and
hugged her. The love of her life, the only man that
she loved and gave her life to was gone. Both her son
and her husband had been taken from her back to
back. She was beyond exhausted and every bone in
her body ached. D-Ball watched from his car and
shook his head. Jamal had seen more tragedy than
anyone he knew and it seemed like he couldn't get a
break to save his life. And now he had to be even
more cautious with the possibility that a target was on
his back. He wasn't sure what kind of men Andre and
Kristoff were, but he knew if Jamal was scared, he'd
better be scared too.

13

After Norman and Braheem's funeral, Jamal was able to convince Denise to go down south until the heat died down and things could get back to normal. He paid for her plane ticket to Sumter, South Carolina and locked her house up.

Jamal was at his apartment taking a look through the file that contained information on Samir's murder. The case was being kept quiet because they were positive that Andre was the murderer. The photo from Samir's surveillance was conclusive that Andre was alive but the problem was that information was never supposed to get out. Andre was a hired assassin sent to the west coast and other parts of the country to carry out hits that higher ups in Law Enforcement were putting out. What Jamal couldn't understand was why was his death faked with the promise that more pressure and focus would be put on Kristoff only to let Kristoff and Samir run rampant for over twenty years? It didn't make sense.

Yani

The lights in his apartment went off and he found himself in total darkness.

"What the hell?" he mumbled to himself. He crawled to the end of the bed and looked out of his window to see if the apartments on the other side of the complex were without power. He stared confused when he saw all of their lights were on with an exception to those who still had not gotten home. He caught a bad feeling and reached in his night stand to get his gun when he felt the barrel of a gun press against the back of his head. He froze in terror.

"You really need to learn to be quicker than that, son," Andre said from behind him. He put the safety back on his gun and took it away.

Jamal swallowed past a knot of fear in his throat as it felt like his heart was going to jump out of his chest. The lights came on and he turned around slowly to look at his father. Andre put his gun in its holster and started sweeping his room with what looked like a metal detector. Jamal watched him wondering what he was doing and why. He heard the buzzing sound off rapidly and loudly underneath a desk up against the wall. Andre reached under it and pulled a tap. Jamal looked at it with wide eyes.

"Looks like somebody's been in here. Did you have company recently?"

"No, I don't bring people to my crib. It's just me and Tiff that lives here," Jamal said as he took the tap from his father and looked it over.

"Your girlfriend?" Andre asked as he stared at his son. He took the tap back and broke it into pieces.

"Yeah," Jamal replied as he shook his head.

"Didn't the last chick you were dealing with help Samir's bitch-ass set you up? You don't think she could do the same thing?"

Jamal thought back to Kareema, the treacherous bitch that almost got him killed. No way was his luck that bad that he ended up with another chick like her. Jamal shook his head, "No, Tiff ain't like that. I would've noticed. I knew something was off with Kareema but I wasn't sure what it was. I don't get that vibe from Tiff. She's a good girl."

Andre stared at his son for a moment and then fixed his eyes on the ring that Jamal still wore around his neck. "But she's not Tamera."

Jamal looked at his father but didn't know what to say. "What are you doing here?" he asked instead.

"I figured you had some questions," Andre started as he sat down at Jamal's desk. "So, ask away."

Jamal had a million and one questions since he first confirmed his father was alive. But seeing him face to face left him speechless. All he could do was stare at the man he never had a chance to get to know. He shook his head feeling dumbfounded. "Damn, we really do look just a like," was all that Jamal could say.

Andre snickered, "The first time I saw you at your college graduation…"

Jamal interrupted him, "You were there?" he asked, completely unaware.

"Yeah, I was there," Andre replied. He cleared his throat. "When I saw you all I could say was: Got damn, ain't no denying this boy. You look like I spit you out my damn self." They chuckled together. Jamal noticed their voices even sound alike.

"Why did you come back?" Jamal asked.

Andre sighed, "Samir was going to kill you. You had so many near misses with him, I knew it was only a matter of time before he caught you coming from an ATM or getting off of work late or coming from getting a haircut and just took you out like that without you even seeing it coming. I wasn't about to let that happen."

"But you had to know that Sa' had security cameras in there," Jamal replied.

"I didn't give a fuck. Whoever wanted fucking trouble they can come see me about it. But that muthafucka wasn't about to add you to his body count. Besides, I knew if the cops saw my pic they weren't going to do shit. Hell, they're the reason I'm who I am. I did them a fucking favor. I did what they were supposed to do twenty fucking years ago," Andre seethed.

"But Kristoff…" Jamal started. He searched his father's face.

"That was a miscalculation on my part. I thought I killed that sonuva bitch."

Jamal stared at his father wide eyed. "That was you…you slit his throat?"

Andre looked at his son with cold, heartless eyes. "I should've cut his whole fucking head off. The shit was supposed to fall back on Samir. I knew that little pussy had police backing him but I didn't realize in all the years I was gone that he had Sergeants, Lieutenants, Captains even fucking judges in his pocket. This nigga had alliances in the fucking mafia."

"The Russian Mafia…" Jamal replied. Andre nodded his head. "Samir knew Kristoff wasn't dead. That's why he was able to gain back territories again. But I thought Kristoff was working with the Columbians."

Andre shook his head. "No son, Kristoff is Russian. No way would he go to bed with the fucking Columbians. That's like Hitler fucking a Jew-bitch; punishable by death.

"Son, you better get up on your job because you don't know half of what the fuck is going on around you. More than half of the fucking Philadelphia Police is run by the Russian Mob. It used to be a split with territories Smitty and the Columbians had, and the territories Kristoff and Samir along with the Russians had. I was a small timer back before you were born, a number runner. But Smitty knew I was more. Yeah he was a cop, but he wasn't like Kristoff on some take over shit. He just was trying to put a little extra money in his pocket to feed his family. Shit, back then, cops weren't getting paid as well as they are now and if you had kids on a cop's salary, forget about it…"

"Get to the point, dad," Jamal said becoming impatient. "How do I stop him now? Because you know and I know that until they get you, they're coming after me next. I'm the only one left besides Shawn. They're picking us off one by fucking one because you didn't do your homework when you went off on your little killing spree!" Jamal said angrily.

"You kill him and as many of them as you can and then you get the fuck outta dodge," Andre replied in a menacing tone.

Jamal shook his head. "You're not understanding; this shit ain't gonna stop because one got knocked off or a few of them. It's the fucking mob!"

"No, you're not understanding. The Philly pigs doesn't consist of the Russian Mob, they are run by it, ruled by it. Blackmail, extortion, fear, all led by one man. You know how many of them want to get from under Kristoff's heel?" Andre said back.

"Okay, if that's the case, why haven't any of them tried to take him out?" Jamal asked.

"Fear is stronger than love, son. Always remember that. Fear will make a muthafucka do some of the strangest things. That's why Kristoff wanted me, because I don't fear shit. You think if you turn the other cheek, they won't come after you? You think if I hadn't come back, they would have ignored your presence? Pay attention, son! Why the fuck do you think they were so eager to get you on the PPD? Because Davidson asked? Man, hell no! Because you're my son. You think your record is expunged? Think again! They know about all of that shit. They know you killed Khalil at fifteen and knowing you have that killer instinct, that fearless, ruthless killer instinct is why they wanted you. The only reason they haven't snatched your ass yet is because I came back. These cops aren't shaking your hand because you're this awesome man of the law. They remember you when you were in stolen cars, knocking muthafuckas out, slinging dope. They know you killed Khalil, they know you killed El. I promise you, they may not want you dead yet. They may try to use you to get to me. But they definitely want you on their side just like they wanted me. Now you can do one of two things; kill that sonuva bitch Kristoff, or pack up your shit and get the fuck outta dodge before they decide that you're better off dead."

Jamal looked at his father speechless. His father knew everything he had ever done. He knew about Khalil, he knew about El. It was starting to make sense to him now why things were going so well for him even in Delaware. Now he really wasn't sure who he could trust. Normally, he was able to make his own decisions, but being near his father left him unable to decide on his next move.

"What do I do, Dad? What do I do, now?" he asked his father.

Andre rose from his chair so he could get ready to leave. "I already told you. The one thing I regret not teaching you before I had to leave is that your life is more valuable than anyone else's. Self-preservation. But even without me teaching you that, you already know. This is no different than when you went up against Samir; kill or be killed. Don't fear no muthafucking man because they bleed just like you do," Andre told his son.

"But how do I get to Kristoff? I've never seen him before. I don't know what he looks like. I don't know shit about him."

"Check your mailbox when I'm gone. Everything you need is in there." Andre tossed a phone to Jamal. "There's one number programmed in that phone. It's untraceable. That's the only number you need to call to reach me. I would suggest you get yourself a metal detector. I know you like this Tiff girl, but don't let your heart or your dick over-rule your head. Check her out and if she so much as has an overdue library book, get rid of her ass."

Jamal couldn't help but to chuckle at what his father said. "I guess you don't know me that well, Pops. I been checked her out. She's clean. Trust me Dad, she's a good girl."

"Alright, if you say so. But that still leaves a problem. If she can't be blackmailed and she can't be bought, she can be killed. History repeats itself for all those who forgot it," Andre said speaking of Tamera.

Jamal lowered his eyes knowing exactly what his dad was talking about. "I know," he said quietly.

"Decide what you're going to do. We have less than 48 hours to make a move against them before they make a move against us."

Before Jamal could respond, the lights went out again. This time he looked out the window and saw that some of the other apartments went dark as well. He grabbed his gun from his night-stand but then twenty seconds later, the lights came back on and his father was gone.

Jamal let out a sigh of relief. "This nigga thinks he's Batman," he said with a chuckle. His cell phone rang and he answered. "Williams."

ATR 3: The Wrath of Andre

"We need you at the station, Jamal. Now." A voice on the other end of the line said with authority.

Jamal hesitated for a moment. "Okay, I'll be there in twenty minutes." Jamal disconnected the call and got up from his bed. He took his shirt off and put on a bullet proof vest. He then grabbed his service revolver and two clips along with his personal gun and two clips. He was tying his sneakers when he heard Tiffany come into the apartment.

"Marco!" she called out.

"Polo, babe! I'm in the bedroom," Jamal replied.

Tiffany came into the room and smiled when she saw Jamal. She sat her shopping bags on the desk and greeted him with a kiss. "Mmm, gimme another one," she said with a smile. Jamal kissed her again. "The craziest thing just happened. I ran into a guy that looked just like you. I mean, he could have been your twin," Tiffany said as she took her jacket off and hung it up.

"Is that right?" Jamal asked as he stood up.

"Yeah. You know what they say; everybody has a twin. Are you heading out?"

"Yeah, the station just called me in. I'm still on leave so I don't think it's work related. Probably about my uncle or my mom," Jamal replied as he wrapped his arms around Tiffany and hugged her.

Tiffany felt the bullet proof vest and looked up at him. "What's with the vest?" she asked.

Jamal hesitated, "It's like a condom, boo; I'd rather have it and not need it, than need it and not have it." He could see the worried expression on her face and gave her another kiss before smacking her on the backside. Tiffany laughed out loud and pulled away.

"I was going to cook some dinner for us. You want some shrimp fettuccini with a salad?" Tiffany asked as she walked into the bathroom and began to undress for a shower. Jamal stared at her before answering. Tiffany was absolutely gorgeous; beautiful, flawless, smooth mahogany skin that reminded him of a Hershey's candy bar, a slender build with long shapely legs, semi-wide hips, a southern round, high backside and firm breasts. The blacker the berry, the sweeter the juice was accurate and she was heavy into Black Empowerment. She wore her hair natural, mostly in a kinky-curly blow out style. He watched as she pinned her hair up while only in her bra and panties and was suddenly filled with lust. Jamal walked behind her and wrapped his arms around her waist before planting a kiss on her neck.

"Whatever you fix tonight, I'm cool with it," he said as he looked at her through the mirror. She smiled as she stared back at him. "You are so beautiful." Tiffany's smile broadened and he kissed the side of her mouth. "I've gotta go."

"Okay," Tiffany replied as she watched him leave out of the bathroom. After he left, she locked the bottom and top lock and put the chain-lock on as well and set the alarm. She also went into the bedroom and lifted her side of the mattress and pulled a .38 caliber pistol that Jamal purchased for her. Though she told him that she wasn't worried, she was well aware of what was going on around him even without him telling her much and she was not going to be caught slipping. She took the gun in the bathroom with her, closed and locked the door and proceeded to take her shower.

13

Jamal walked into the station. After the conversation that he had with his father, everybody was suspicious to him. The first person he saw was Pete. Pete looked extremely nervous and motioned for Jamal to come over to him.

"What's good, Pete?" Jamal greeted his friend with a handshake.

Pete spoke in a low tone. "IAB is in there waiting to speak with you. They know you requested the file. They tried to shake me down but I didn't tell them anything, mostly because I didn't know anything. I don't know what the hell is going on, but they don't seem too pleased with you. Almost as if they want to nail your ass for some shit. Watch yourself when you go in there," Pete warned.

Jamal looked over towards the interrogation room and noticed two plain clothes cops were watching him. He nodded at Pete and went over to his desk as if he didn't know what was going on. One of the officers who was staring at Jamal walked over to him.

He was a little shorter than Jamal with a medium build, dirty blonde hair with a part on the left side and a square jaw. He stared at Jamal with a smug look on his face as he tucked his thumbs inside of his belt and stood next to Jamal's desk.

"Can I help you with something?" Jamal asked the officer.

The officer stared down at Jamal trying to be intimidating as he twirled a toothpick in his mouth. Jamal was not fazed by his behavior. "Lieutenant wants you in interrogation room 1, now. Move your ass."

Jamal stood straight up and looked the officer dead in the eye. "Do you have a problem?"

"You better check your tone, boy," the officer said as he stood closer to Jamal.

"I'm a grown-ass man, get that shit straight. If you got a fucking problem, come at me correct and don't come in my face with the nut-shit 'cause I won't hesitate to knock you smooth the fuck out," Jamal said in a loud and threatening tone, drawing attention. Pete looked over at them and stood up just in case anything jumped off.

"Williams!" Jamal heard his Lieutenant call to him. "Get in here, now! Bradley, this doesn't concern you. Get back to work before you find yourself on the tail end of a suspension."

Bradley looked at the Lieutenant and then eye-balled Jamal. He walked past Jamal close enough to bump him but didn't touch him.

"Yeah, you fucking knew better. Don't get yourself fucked up in here," Jamal warned him.

Bradley turned around. "You know, you're nothing but a street punk! You wanna go, we can take it outside!" he said as he snatched the toothpick from his mouth and threw it to the floor.

"Williams and Bradley! Either cut the shit out or you'll both be stepping outside and headed over to the unemployment line!" the Lieutenant said, giving them a final warning. If looks could kill, the look Jamal gave Bradley would have put him into a premature grave. Bradley turned to go about his business as Jamal headed over to the interrogation room. He sat down in a chair and the Lieutenant closed the door behind him. There were two more plain clothes cops in the room as well. Jamal looked them all over and caught a bad feeling. The room was silent so Jamal decided to speak first.

ATR 3: The Wrath of Andre

"If this is a party, where's the chips and beer? Otherwise, why am I being called in here while I'm supposed to be on family leave?" Jamal asked as he leaned back in his chair and crossed his arms over his chest.

One of the plain clothes cops tossed a folder onto the table in front of Jamal. "You requested information on the murder of Samir Muhammad, a case that has a pretty tight lid on it. Any particular reason why?"

Jamal looked at him and frowned. "He was my cousin and he was murdered…why wouldn't I want to know how the investigation is going?"

The officers looked at each other and then looked at Jamal. "Samir Muhammad tried to kill you numerous times, was suspected in the murder of numerous friends of yours as well as your former girlfriend, Tamera Harrison, and you suddenly felt so remorseful over his murder that you wanted to keep tabs on the investigation? I call bullshit on that," another plain clothes officer said as he half-way sat on the edge of the table.

"You can call it what you want. Regardless of what went on between us, he was still my cousin and I would have rather he was brought up on charges that would actually stick than have him gunned down the way he was," Jamal partially lied.

"We pulled some images from Muhammad's security cam. We want you to look at them and tell us if you recognize the person in the photos," the Lieutenant said to Jamal.

Jamal looked at everyone in the room and then looked at the folder. He didn't need to look inside as he had already seen the photos of his father. He stalled wondering what his reaction should be. He opened the folder and looked through the pictures casually and then shrugged his shoulders. "I don't recognize this man," he lied.

One of the officers laughed a hearty laugh, "Bullshit Jamal, look again. Look real closely. Take all the damn time you need."

"Look, I don't know what you're getting at, but I don't know who the hell this is," Jamal said back.

"You're telling me you don't recognize your old man when you see him? The sonuva bitch looks identical to you," the same officer said as he snatched up one of the photos.

"Sorry to burst your bubble, Dennis, but I didn't grow up with my father. Never saw him, never met him," Jamal lied with a straight face as he looked Dennis in the eyes.

"Careful Jamal, you're walking a fine line right now," his Lieutenant warned.

"And what's that supposed to mean?" Jamal asked.

"Let's talk about the night of your mother's shooting," Dennis suggested.

"Yeah, what about it?" Jamal asked.

"You told Officer Gomez that you and your mother were talking when a man came through the back, which you shot…"

"Yeah…" Jamal replied.

"And he got off a shot which hit your mother in the back…" the officer continued.

"Yeah…" Jamal said again.

"Then you said someone came through the front and you shot them and two others came through the back and you shot them as well."

"Yeah, that's what I said," Jamal said as he shrugged his shoulders.

"Ahh see, that is where we have the problem. Your gun is a Beretta service revolver. We found two slugs from your weapon in only one of the perps found in the kitchen. The other two along with the one who came in through the front had .44 slugs in them," Dennis said.

"Maybe they shot each other," Jamal replied.

"That could very well be the case if they weren't both carrying 9MM pistols," Dennis said as he leaned closer to Jamal.

Jamal was silent for a moment. "I don't know what to tell you."

"Jamal, we know that someone else was in that house with you. We have a witness who stated they saw a man leave out the back of your mother's house no less than five minutes after the shots stopped, climbed onto the roof and disappeared. You know who this was. Who are you protecting?" the Lieutenant asked.

"Nobody," Jamal said with a straight face.

"Bullshit Jamal! Come on!"

"Look, what the hell do y'all want me to say? Someone is targeting my family. Two of my cousins are dead, my uncle is dead, my mother was shot and I could have been killed, too. Y'all in here showing me pictures claiming it's a man that's been dead for more than twenty years…"

Dennis put his hand up to silence Jamal. "Wait a minute now. For someone who never saw and never met the man, how do you figure he's dead?"

"You ass-hole, that's why I never saw and never met the man because he was murdered. Killed back in 1987 at the hands of my own fucking cousin while one of your own stood there and watched and didn't do a fucking thing about it. Samir killed my father right in front of my mother with Kristoff right fucking there and had her living in fear all this time. I don't know who the fuck that is in the photo, but it damn sure isn't my father because the man is dead. And unless the reality I'm used to has changed, the nigga didn't rise from the dead to get revenge like he's fucking Brandon Lee and this is The fucking Crow!" Jamal ranted before standing up from his chair in such a fury that he knocked the chair over.

"Okay Jamal, calm down," the Lieutenant said with his hands up sensing Jamal's hostility.

"Nah fuck this! I just buried my cousin and my uncle. My aunt is going bat shit outta her mind not to mention my mother is in a fucking hospital lucky to be alive and lucky to not be paralyzed, and instead of you muthafuckas going out and finding whoever this is that's targeting my family, y'all are trying to indicate I know shit or I'm fucking hiding shit. What the fuck part of being a cop is this?" Jamal was heated but playing the role of the victim very well. His reaction was believable to his lieutenant but Dennis wasn't buying it.

"Okay Jamal, listen, we're not trying to insinuate anything, okay. We're just trying to get to the bottom of all of this," the Lieutenant tried to reassure Jamal.

"You wanna get to the bottom of this? Find out who murdered my cousin and then kidnapped his son and killed my uncle. Do your job and get the fuck off my back! Are we done?" Jamal asked.

The room was silent so Jamal walked over to the door.

"Jamal, I hope for your sake you aren't lying. It's not a good look for a cop to be covering for a murderer," Dennis said. Jamal looked Dennis up and down and then stormed out of the room. Pete looked at him confused.

"Jamal, is everything okay?" Pete asked.

Jamal didn't respond. He snatched his jacket up and left the precinct to head back to his apartment.

"He's lying," Dennis said to the Lieutenant.

"Yeah, I know. He knows Andre is alive. The problem is; is he protecting him or working with him?" the Lieutenant asked as he rubbed the hairs on his chin.

"It's no telling how much he knows if Andre made contact with him. Bottom line is Kristoff wants Andre dead at any costs. He should've surfaced by now." Dennis replied. "Killing his brother wasn't enough. We're going to have to hit a little closer to home."

"Not just yet. Let's see if Jamal leads us to Andre. The tap in his apartment was destroyed. Put eyes on his apartment. If need be, take his girlfriend. Maybe the fear that history is repeating itself will make Jamal more inclined to bring his father in."

Pete was making copies near the interrogation room that Dennis and the Lieutenant were in and overheard everything. He quietly went back to his desk feeling uneasy. He always suspected that there were dirty cops on the force but never imagined they would kill one of their own. He wanted to warn Jamal to watch his back but didn't want to jeopardize himself. What was he going to do?

14

Jamal made it back to his apartment but couldn't get the door opened due to the chain-lock being on.

"Babe, open the door, it's me." Jamal called to Tiffany.

Tiffany had just begun to nod off when she heard Jamal's voice. She tucked the gun back under the bed and went over to the door wearing nothing but a satin royal blue robe and matching royal blue panties and bra. She put her arm up and leaned onto the wall as she peered out at Jamal.

"What's the magic words?" she asked seductively.

Jamal chuckled. "Please?" he asked sweetly.

Tiffany opened the door for him and could immediately tell that he was upset. "Babe, what's wrong?" she asked him.

Jamal shook his head as he wrapped his arms around her and hugged her tightly.

ATR 3: The Wrath of Andre

"Are you hungry? I left the oven on so your food would stay warm."

Jamal let her go. "Yeah, I could use a grub right now." Tiffany disappeared into the kitchen while Jamal went into their bedroom and took his sneakers off. He sat on the edge of the bed and thought over the interrogation that the cops gave him while he was at the station. They were onto Andre and they suspected he was involved with his father. Jamal's only questions were if they simply wanted to bring him in for the murder of Samir or if they were trying to get him to Kristoff. He played with Tamera's ring that hung around his neck as he sat thinking. When he heard Tiffany coming into their bedroom, he kissed the ring and let it fall back against his chest.

"Thanks babe," Jamal said as she sat the tray in front of him. They talked while Jamal ate. When he was finished, Tiffany took his dishes back to the kitchen and placed them in the dishwasher. Jamal was undressing so he could take a shower when she returned.

Jamal took her by the hand as he backed towards their bathroom. "Come take a shower with me," he said with a grin.

Tiffany grinned with him. "And then what?" she asked as she followed him.

Jamal slid her robe from off of her after they made it to the bathroom. "I'm thinking we should aim for a gold medal in the Hugh Hefner Olympics." Tiffany burst out laughing while Jamal turned the shower water on making sure it was hot like the both of them liked it. He snatched her close to him making her gasp. Her heart began to race when Jamal kissed her slowly and deeply. He ran his fingers through her thick hair as her fingers danced around the bottom of his shirt. She pulled away from him just long enough to pull his shirt over his head. Jamal unfastened the bullet proof vest and tossed it out of the bathroom where it landed on the hallway floor. Tiffany traced her fingers over his abs before sliding her hands to his back, squeezing him as he kissed and nibbled on her neck while unclasping her bra. He slid her arms out of it before cupping her firm breasts in his hands, gently squeezing them before rolling his thumbs over her pearly, dark nipples. Jamal backed her against their sink as he kissed her deeply, their tongues dancing against one another as if in a sword match. Tiffany lift herself up onto the sink and wrapped her legs around Jamal as he kissed from her chin down to her neck before squeezing her large breasts together and flickering his tongue over her hardened nipples. Tiffany leaned her head back and closed her eyes, loving the sensation she felt from his warm, wet tongue against her skin. Her moistened kitten purred and throbbed wanting Jamal's erection to stroke her deeply. She reached for his boxers and began to pull them down so she could touch his erection which was hot and throbbing. Jamal moved her hands away and knelt in front of her. He kissed her bare abdomen as he looked up at her while pulling down her panties. Tiffany whimpered when she felt his warm, soft lips brush against her inner thigh as he planted kisses on her. He spread her open to taste her wetness, letting the tip of his tongue dance around the hood of her clit, sucking and licking, before pushing his tongue deeper inside of her. Tiffany cried out in ecstasy as she massaged the back of his head. Jamal continued to lick and suck her clit as if his tongue was a paint brush and her wetness was his easel. Tiffany beat her hand against the sink as her toes curled and she moaned loudly before exploding. Jamal continued to lick and suck on her but Tiffany tapped out.

"Stop, stop, stop," she moaned, out of breath. Jamal laughed as she trembled. Tiffany shook her head at him smiling. "That's not funny." Jamal kissed her and then pulled her into the shower with him.

Tiffany washed his back, marveling over his gorgeous body. Though she had not told Jamal out of fear that her feelings wouldn't be returned, she had fallen deeply for him. She had never come across a man who could touch her mentally and make her feel incredibly beautiful just by the way he looked at her. She was overwhelmed with joy as she traced her fingers over his back and fought hard to keep her tears in. With everything she had experienced in her life and all of her past failed relationships, Jamal just felt too good to be true. If he did turn out to be too good to be true, Tiffany hoped to enjoy him for as long as possible.

They took turns washing each other and then stood under the water making out. Tiffany purposely let the water run in her face to blend in with her tears but Jamal could tell by the way she shivered in his arms that something was wrong.

He turned the water off and passed Tiffany a towel after wrapping one around his waist and they retreated back to their bedroom. After drying off, he laid across the bed and watched Tiffany dry and treat her hair. She rubbed lotion on her body and then joined Jamal under the covers. He put his arm around her as she snuggled close to him and kissed her forehead. He could still feel her shivering.

"You want me to turn the heat up?" he asked her.

"No, I'm okay," Tiffany whispered. She tried to discreetly wipe a tear from her eye but Jamal saw her.

"Talk to me, babe. What's wrong?"

"Nothing," Tiffany replied trying to sound as convincing as possible.

"Don't lie to me, Tiff. Talk to me. What's up?" he asked again.

Tiffany hesitated, thinking of what to say. She didn't want to scare him away. She took a deep breath and figured what the hell; she might as well spit it out. "I have never been this happy before in my whole life. This is the first time where I've felt free, where I can be me and not have to wear a mask or hide who I am or how I feel. I feel peace when I'm with you."

Jamal was quiet for a moment as he played with her hair. "You love me, baby?" he asked her.

"Do you love me?" Tiffany asked nervously.

"I asked you first."

"I asked you second," Tiffany mocked. They giggled together and then fell silent. "Well…?" Tiffany asked as she looked up at him.

Jamal stared at her for a moment. He knew he felt something for her but he wasn't ready to actually say he loved her. "What I feel for you is stronger than anything I've felt for anyone in a long time. I know you want to hear me actually say I love you, but if I said it right now at this moment, it wouldn't be fair to you because of how it came out, you feel me? When I tell I love you, I don't want it to be because that's what you want to hear or that's what you expect me to say. I want it to be a day when I'm looking at you and I'm seeing you as the woman I love and care for and want to spend as much of my life that I'm allowed to spend with you. When I tell you, I want you to feel it, believe it and never second guess it."

Tiffany bit her bottom lip and nodded her head before lying back on his chest. "It feels like you just did," she said softly. Jamal smiled knowing that she would get it. "I love you, too."

15

Pete knew if he could go to anyone about what he heard at the police station, he could go to his father, who was a retired Lieutenant from the 18nd District. Upon bringing the news to his father's attention, he learned much more about Kristoff and Andre than he bargained. His father was well aware of Andre's faked death and the assignments he was placed on across the country as he was the cop in charge of the details. He also was the cop who helped Andre go rogue when he made his decision to come back to Philly to protect his sons. Not feeling that he could trust any of the other officers, he let the ones who were also a part of the special assignment believe that Andre simply dropped off the radar.

A package of information had been put together for Andre once Pete informed his father that Jamal was being targeted as a means to bring Andre in. The package was given to Pete, who discreetly placed it with some of his other items and went to

Jamal's apartment to give it to him. He was instructed by his father to never speak with Jamal over the phone about anything that was going on, assuming that his calls were tapped.

Jamal answered the intercom to his apartment. "Yo!"

"Hey Jamal, this is Pete. I need to come up to see you. I have something for you," Pete said through the speaker.

Jamal hesitated, still not sure as to who he could trust. "Now's not a good time, homie. I'm a little busy right now."

Pete sighed trying to find a way to say what he needed to say. "I need to give you what Katie couldn't find on her own. Trust me; you need to let me up."

Jamal tapped his fingers and then buzzed Pete up. He stood in the bedroom doorway and watched Tiffany asleep in the bed with the sheets clinging to her body while he waited for Pete to make his way up to his apartment. When he heard Pete knock on the door, he took his gun from his desk drawer and gave Tiffany a soft kiss on her forehead. She stirred but didn't wake. Jamal closed their bedroom door and opened the door to their apartment to let Pete in.

After closing the door, Jamal looked at him for a moment. "Not to sound paranoid or anything, but lift your shirt, homie."

Pete looked at him confused. "What? Why?"

"I need to make sure they didn't send you in here on some mole shit. Lift your shirt," Jamal instructed him.

"Are you kidding me? You think I'm wired? I came over here on my own free will. Nobody wired me and sent me on some double agent shit," Pete smirked.

"Then you won't have a problem lifting your shirt," Jamal replied with a serious expression that let Pete know he was not joking.

Pete huffed and shook his head as he pulled his shirt out of his pants and lift it up. "You happy now?" he asked as he turned around to show Jamal he wasn't wired. "Need me to take my pants off too?"

"Nah homie," Jamal walked over to Pete and frisked him just to be sure.

"This is ridiculous. I thought we were better than this!" Pete scoffed.

"Yeah well with all the shit I've seen in the last few weeks, a nigga can't be too sure these days." When Jamal was satisfied, he motioned for Pete to follow him to the living room. He did like his father said and got a portable metal detector and did a sweep of his apartment every day whenever he left and came back in to make sure no more taps were in. They sat down at the kitchen table. "You want something to drink or to eat?" Jamal offered.

"No I'm fine. I don't want to stay too long. I just wanted to give you this," Pete reached inside of his black bag and pulled the package that his father gave to him. "You need to get this to Andre, your father, as soon as possible."

Jamal was about to take a drink from his cup of orange juice and stopped. He stared at Pete for a moment without saying anything.

"I know you're wondering how I know. All I can tell you is that my father along with some other higher ups from the 80's helped your father fake his death to avoid murder charges and to have him help bring down Kristoff. Your father is…was a hired gun until he dropped off the radar. He kept in contact with my father because my father was supplying him with the info that he needed to carry out the hits he needed to carry out in Philly in part to pin evidence on Samir Muhammad and in part to protect you and Shawn…"

Jamal interrupted him, "Wait, wait, wait. Wait a fucking minute…"

"Jamal, listen to me. I don't have a lot of time. They needed Kristoff and your cousin Samir to believe your father was dead to take the focus off of him in hopes they could get Kristoff for drug trafficking, extortion, murder, something! But with him having ties to the Russian Mob and using small timers to handle his dirty work, his hands never got dirty. Your father got frustrated because he wasn't expecting it to take as long as it was taking and then you got caught up in the shit, so he basically said fuck it and went rogue.

"This shit with dirty cops and Kristoff spread like the fucking plague. My father can't tell who's on what side. But he still has connections and was able to pull info on Kristoff and five of his major players, two of which are cops. One is a captain with IAB right here in Philly and another is a Lieutenant Sheila Armstrong in Delaware," Pete said as he slid one of the papers out and glanced at it.

Jamal froze. "What?" he asked Pete as his heart raced in his chest. "Let me see that." Jamal said as he held his hand out. Pete handed him the package and Jamal pulled the paper work out. He stared with his mouth partially hanging open at the page listing the major players in Kristoff's operation. Sheila Armstrong was his former Lieutenant when he worked with the Wilmington Delaware Police Department. She practically took him under her wing when he graduated from the police academy. All that time he worked under her, she more than likely was keeping tabs on him for Kristoff and whoever else.

"You've gotta be fucking kidding me…" Jamal mumbled as he stared at her photo.

"There's more Jamal," Pete said, snapping Jamal out of his thoughts. "The other day when you came into the station and had that little dispute with Bradley before you went to talk to Lieutenant Jackson and Dennis; when you left, I overheard Dennis and Jackson talking. They're in on this too and are trying to find a way to get your father to resurface where they can actually get their hands on him. They want you to lead them to him…even if it means using your girlfriend as leverage. You need to get her out of here."

ATR 3: The Wrath of Andre

"You heard them say that after I left?" Jamal asked Pete.

"Right after you stormed out, I went to go make copies of a police report I was writing up and I heard them talking. They said something about killing your uncle and your cousin wasn't enough."

Jamal felt a heated fury rising within him. Everything in his body made him want to go to the police station and start dishing out head shots. He leaned onto the table and hung his head to keep from verbalizing his thoughts of violence and revenge. "If those pussies were behind killing my uncle and my cousin; that means those muthafuckas were behind shooting my mom. All bets are fucking off."

"Jamal wait, don't do anything stupid," Pete insisted.

"Fuck that! This shit just turned from business to fucking personal. It's bad enough they came for my uncle, but they brought the bullshit to my mother's door step. It's a fucking wrap…" Jamal hushed when he saw Tiffany come into the kitchen.

"Babe, what's going on? I heard you in my sleep. Is everything okay?" she asked as she glanced from Pete back to Jamal.

Pete stood up quickly and grabbed his bag. "I'll be in touch, Jamal. Remember what I said," Pete said firmly. Jamal nodded his head but didn't respond. Pete smiled at Tiffany and then Jamal walked him to the door to let him out. He locked up behind him and joined Tiffany in the kitchen.

"What is going on?" Tiffany asked him again as she looked him over. Besides hearing the hostility in his voice that woke her from her sleep, she could see in his face that something had pissed him off entirely.

Jamal took the package, refusing to look at her and shook his head. "Nothing," he said flatly.

Tiffany stood next to him and stared at him as she tapped her fingers on the table. She then placed her hands on his face and made him look at her. "Baby, I don't do well with secrets. Something is obviously wrong that had you in here snapping. Talk to me."

Jamal looked her in the eyes as he thought of what Pete told him that he overheard at the precinct. He grabbed her hand and kissed her palm. "I need you to go stay with your Aunt in New York for a little while."

Tiffany looked at him wide eyed. "What?! Why?"

"Because this shit that's going on with my family isn't over and I don't want you to get hurt,"

"But Jamal…" Tiffany started.

Jamal shushed her. "Don't debate me, Tiff. I can't let history repeat itself. I can't handle losing you, too. I need you to do this for me."

Tiffany searched his face, trying to pick her words carefully. "If I leave, history will already begin to repeat itself. You don't have eyes over in New York. So if you're telling me to go there, that leaves me unprotected and if this thing that's going on with you and your family is as bad as you think it is, I'm safer with you. I would feel safer with you. I would feel better knowing I'm with you."

Jamal shook his head. "I don't want what happened to Tammy to happen to you."

"I'm not Tammy, Jamal. Nothing is going to happen to me. But if you send me away calling yourself hiding me like you tried to hide Tammy and your brother…" Jamal closed his eyes feeling the pain from Tamera's murder all over again. Tiffany stood on her tippy toes and kissed him softly. "History will

already begin to repeat itself if you send me away,"
she said again.

Jamal thought over what she said and
partially believed she was right. He didn't have eyes
over in New York and it was him and his father
against who knows how many. At least in Philly he
had D-Ball, Pete and his father. He sat down in the
kitchen chair and pulled Tiffany between his legs.

"Is your license to carry still here?" he asked
her.

"Yes, I keep it in my handbag with my
driver's license. Why?"

"Where's the holster I bought for you?"

"In the dresser drawer, I believe." Tiffany
replied, catching on.

"You carry that gun with you at all times.
You remember what I taught you, remember what I
told you."

"I know," Tiffany said. "Shoot to kill, not to
injure because the other person may not have given
me the same courtesy."

Jamal nodded his head and then kissed her
chin. He stared at her for a moment, loving
everything about her. History was not going to repeat
itself.

"You want some breakfast?" Tiffany asked him.

"Of course," Jamal smiled.

Tiffany smiled back at him. "Let me go get cleaned up and I'ma hook you up." She pulled away from him and Jamal smacked her on her backside making her giggle. "Freak!" she hollered as she skipped down the hallway to the bathroom. Jamal felt his back pocket vibrate and pulled the phone his father gave him from it.

"Hello?" Jamal answered.

"Denise's house, twenty minutes," Andre said and then disconnected the call.

Jamal looked at the phone and then closed his eyes. "Babe!" he called out to Tiffany.

"Yes," she answered with her mouth full of toothpaste and water.

"I've gotta make a run real fast so I'ma just pick something up for us at that diner you like. You want the French toast or the blueberry pancakes with bacon and scrambled cheese eggs?" Jamal asked as he went to their bedroom to put on his bullet proof vest and another shirt.

Yani

Tiffany gargled and then spat in the toilet before rinsing her mouth out. "Where are you going?" she asked as she wiped her mouth on her wash cloth.

"Police business, boop," Jamal replied as he checked his gun to make sure it was fully loaded and then chambered a round. He tucked it in his holster and sat down to put his sneakers on.

"I thought you were still on leave."

"I am, but this is something I'm doing on my own. I can't really go into details. It's just something I need to do because I don't want to just depend on the force to handle everything that's going on." He finished tying his shoes and then checked to make sure he had everything. He then remembered the package that Pete told him to give to his father and went into the kitchen to retrieve it. Tiffany followed behind him.

"French toast, scrambled cheese eggs and bacon is fine," she said to him as she walked him to the door.

"Okay. I won't be gone long," Jamal told her as he hugged her tightly. He gave her a long, wet kiss. "I love you," he told her before giving her another peck on the lips.

Tiffany smiled and kissed him back. "I love you, too." Jamal left out and she locked the door behind him, put the chain-lock on and set the alarm.

Jamal went to his car and called D-Ball.

"Yo homie, what's up?" D-Ball answered after the second ring.

"Nothing much, what's good with you?" Jamal asked as he backed out of his parking spot and began driving to his aunt's house.

"Chilling on my day off. Liz is at work so it's kinda quiet in here."

"I need a favor, D-Ball."

"What's up?" D-Ball asked as he flipped through the television channels.

"I need you to swing by my apartment complex and keep an eye on Tiff for me. Just say your computer is down and I said you could use my laptop. I'ma send her a text to let her know you're on your way."

"Is everything alright?" D-Ball asked as he got up from his bed to put his shoes on.

"I can't get into it right now. All I'ma say is I don't want history to repeat itself, feel me?"

D-Ball caught on. "Say no more. I'm on my way."

Yani

"Thanks homie," Jamal disconnected the call and waited until he got to the next red light to send Tiffany the text message. Just as the light was changing to green, she responded saying "ok". Jamal sat his phone to the side and started driving again. He noticed for three blocks that the same black Marauder was following him. At first he thought maybe it was his father but when he glanced in his rearview mirror, he could tell there were two people in the car and they didn't appear to be Black.

"Can you muthafuckas be any more obvious?" Jamal said to himself. He made a left turn and wasn't surprised that the Marauder made a left turn with him. He then made a right turn and just as he expected them to, they made a right turn as well. "Oh, I see how y'all niggas wanna play." Jamal reached in his glove compartment and pulled out his glock 9 with hollow tip bullets as he pulled up to make a left turn from Old York Road to Stenton Avenue. He wasn't surprised that the car did the same. When the light turned green, instead of making his turn, he sat there. A few other cars were behind the one following him, also wanting to make a left turn and began honking their horns. Jamal tapped his steering wheel patiently and then sped off to do his left turn just as the light turned red. The Marauder tried to do the same but had to swerve out of the way of a trash truck. Jamal laughed to himself as he sped down Stenton Avenue. He barely made it through a yellow light and when he got to the corner of Ogontz and Stenton Avenues, he noticed the 6 bus was about to cross through the green light. He looked in his rear view mirror and noticed the Marauder was coming up Stenton Avenue, two blocks behind him. Jamal made a quick right turn before the 6 bus made it through the intersection. Though he was partially laughing to himself, he knew being followed was no laughing matter and tried a little harder to shake the tail. As he was crossing through 66th and Ogontz Avenue, he looked in his rearview mirror again to see that the 6 bus was pulling over to let some of the passengers off and pick some more up. The light was turning yellow and he hoped that it turned red, but the Marauder sped around the bus and jumped the light.

"Muthafucka," Jamal mumbled. He thought of the different places where he could stop not wanting to lead whoever that was to his aunt's house and his father. He then thought of the barbershop where his uncle was taken and drove over to Tulpehocken. The Marauder was unable to jump another red light because two cop cars were on the corner of Andrews and Ogontz Avenue by the gas station. As Jamal approached the corner of Tulpehocken, he saw that there was a parking spot in front of the barbershop. He busted a quick U-turn and quickly parallel parked. As he was throwing change into the meter, he noticed the Marauder coming his way. He pretended as if he didn't see them before they got close enough and went inside of the barbershop.

"Hey Skip," Jamal spoke as he gave the barber a handshake.

"How you been Jamal?" Skip replied.

"I've been good, I've been good," Jamal said quickly as he looked around. He was grateful that it wasn't too crowded. He said to Skip in a low voice, "Listen, I got a tail on me and they just drove by. Does your back way still lead over to Limekiln Pike?"

"Yeah, why what's up?" Skip asked in the same low tone.

"Put me in the chair like you're about to give me a cut and then in like ten minutes, I'ma use your bathroom but leave out the back," Jamal said to him.

"You got heat, Jamal?" Rez asked. "Because you know we ride for ours."

"Nothing I can't handle Rez, but I appreciate it." Jamal sat in the chair and Skip prepped him as if he was giving him a shape up. Jamal peered out the corner of his eye and notice two white guys walking by the barbershop slowly before going on their way. Rez noticed them too.

"I think they just made you," Rez said as he followed the two guys with his eyes.

"Yeah I wanted them to," Jamal said.

"Ay yo Boston, come here real quick!" Rez said to a guy in the back. A young slender guy who didn't look any older than twenty years old came to the front of the shop.

"What's up, Rez?" Boston spoke. Jamal could tell by his accent that was the reason he was called Boston.

"Take the broom and go out front. I want you to sweep the pavement. There are two white dudes that just walked by. If they're just standing around, drop the broom. Don't be all obvious and Joe about it. But if they get in a car but don't drive off, just bend down and tie your shoe. Can you handle that?" Rez said to Boston.

"I got it." Boston grabbed the broom and went out front to do as he was told. He swept for about five minutes, making sure he did the curb so he would have an excuse to look in the direction where the two men were. When he noticed they were just casually standing outside, smoking a cigarette, he pretended to trip over the curb and dropped the broom.

"Shit," Jamal said.

"Go, Jamal. Get the fuck outta here before they try some slick shit," Rez told him.

Jamal got up from the chair and slapped Skip and Rez handshakes. "That blue-green Infiniti out there is mine. Throw some change in the meter so I don't get a ticket," Jamal said before making his way to the back. Rez was tall, heavy set and intimidating looking. He grabbed a dust pan and stood in the doorway to block the view so Jamal could head out the back. Jamal went into the bathroom and opened the back window. He climbed out and partially hung from the window sill before pushing off so he could jump the fence across from him. He leaped over and then cut around the back of Limekiln Pike and made his way over to his aunt's house.

"Don't just sweep that shit in the street, use the dust pan," Rez said to Boston when he noticed the two white guys walking back in their direction ten minutes after Jamal left out the back. As he was handing Boston the dust pan, the two guys went into the shop.

"Excuse me, how much for a close fade?" one of the guys asked politely as he casually glanced around.

"Fifteen bucks, my man," Skip said blandly.

"Is there a long wait?" the other guy asked, also glancing around.

"About ten minutes," Skip replied in the same tone.

"Alright, thanks." They left out of the shop and walked past Boston.

"Where the fuck did he go?" Boston heard one ask the other.

"Probably went out the back way."

Boston waited until they went to their car before he swept the rest of the trash into the dust pan and dumped it in a small bag. He then came back inside and said quietly, "I think they know he left out the back."

"Doesn't matter. Fast as Jamal is, he's wherever the hell he needed to go," Skip said.

Rez shook his head. "This shit is fucking crazy."

Jamal ran over to his aunt's house which was eight blocks from the barbershop. He went around back and climbed the fence like he used to when he and Shawn were younger and forgot their keys. Braheem's old bedroom window was unlocked. He lifted it and climbed inside. His father was sitting in a chair holding a gun.

"Oh shit!" Jamal exclaimed, not expecting his dad to be in the room.

"You're late," his father said to him.

"I had a tail," Jamal explained.

Andre stood and moved over to the window, peeking out. "Did you bring them here?"

"No, I ditched them at the barbershop where they took Uncle Norm. My car is still out there but Skip and Rez let me leave out the back." Jamal leaned over, out of breath.

Andre stared out the window a moment longer and then looked at his son. "Next time, use the garage. Norman never fixed the lock."

"How'd you know I would come through here?" Jamal asked.

ATR 3: The Wrath of Andre

Andre shrugged, "It's how I came in the first time I made contact with Norman. Like father, like son."

Jamal suppressed a smile and reached in the bag he was carrying. He pulled out the package that was given to him by Pete. "I was told to give this to you."

"I know. That's why I called you. It's good you checked Pete to see if he was wired. But you never noticed the eye-glasses hanging from his shirt," Andre said as he opened the envelope and pulled out what he needed. Jamal looked at his father confused. Andre noticed the look his son gave him and smiled while shaking his head. "Man, you kids today need to get up on that real modern day technology and stop fucking with that Android and iPhone bullshit. What you thought were ordinary reading glasses was really a mini camera with the recording lens embedded in the eyeglass lens."

"Pete doesn't wear eyeglasses," Jamal said to himself.

"Bingo," Andre said as he looked over the paper work briefly before tucking it in his own bag. "Okay, thanks Jamal. I'll be in touch."

Jamal looked at his father confused again. "Wait a minute…what? That's it?"

"Yeah, that's it."

"Ain't this about a bitch? I just risked my ass to get over here and you're saying it was just so I could play errand boy?! At least tell me what the next move is?" Jamal said as he followed his father out of the room.

"The next move for you is to go back home like you never saw me and wait for me to make contact," Andre said firmly.

"How the hell am I supposed to get out of here without being seen?" Jamal asked as he threw his hands in the air.

Andre turned back to his son. "Jamal, you're not slow. Don't let me coming back prohibit your ability to think on your feet. Be creative. You know damn well you can't just walk out the front door." Andre went down to the kitchen to make himself a sandwich.

Jamal stood in the middle of the room looking around thinking. There weren't a lot of people he could trust at this moment. He didn't want to pull D-Ball off of Tiffany and he didn't want Pete to get any more involved than he already was. He then had a hunch to call Maurice.

"Yo nigga, what's up?" Maurice greeted on the phone.

"Hey Mar, what's going on?" Jamal spoke into the phone.

"I just got back in the crib from Deisha's doctor's appointment."

"Oh yeah? Y'all find out what y'all having?" Jamal asked. Deisha and Maurice had married in June 2012 and were expecting their first child. Maurice couldn't be happier or more proud.

"Yeah, it's a boy. Lil' Mar-Mar junior," Maurice said proudly.

"That's what's up. Congratulations. How's the misses anyway?" Jamal asked as he paced back and forth in the room.

"She's good. Still working. You know how Deisha is. How's everything with the fam?"

"Shit is still crazy but I'ma have to get into that another time. Look I need a favor. You think you can come pick me up?"

"Yeah, where you at? Your car broke down or something?" Maurice asked.

"Something like that. Remember where I took you, Deisha and Chanda that summer to see Shawn and Tammy?" Jamal asked, hoping Maurice would catch on. Maurice thought for a moment and caught on.

"Yeah, I remember. I'm on my way." Maurice said as he grabbed his keys.

"Come around the back way," Jamal instructed.

"Alright, I'll be there." Jamal disconnected the call. He then rubbed his hands over his face as he thought of how to get his car from in front of the barbershop. He then remembered his friend Antoine that had a tow truck. He called him next and had him pick his car up from in front of the barbershop and tow it to his apartment complex. Afterwards, he called Skip at the barbershop to let him know his car was about to be towed so they weren't alarmed. Skip informed him that the guys left twenty minutes after he did. Jamal thanked him for his help and then disconnected the call.

Instead of saying goodbye to his father, he left out the basement and peeked out of the window for Maurice's Dodge Charger. He sent him a message letting him know to text him when he got to the back of the house. Twenty minutes later, Maurice replied to let him know he was there. Jamal saw when the Charger backed into the driveway. He crept out the back and made his way over to the back of the car, crouched down. He signaled for Maurice to unlock the back door and he climbed inside and stayed low.

"Yo, what the hell is going on?" Maurice asked.

"I can't explain, just get me the hell outta here and back to my apartment," Jamal said as he stayed low so he couldn't be seen. Maurice waited a moment and then pulled out of the driveway and made his way back to Jamal's apartment. "Make sure you don't have a tail," Jamal instructed.

"Naw, we're good." Maurice said. He zigged in and out of traffic to get Jamal home as quick as possible.

Jamal sat up and let out a deep sigh. He shook his head, "Man this shit is crazy."

"What the hell is up? You out here in your 007 bag and shit," Maurice half-way joked.

"Man it's too much to get into. And honestly, the less you know the better."

"Does this have to do with what happened with your uncle?" Maurice asked.

"Yeah," Jamal replied. Maurice looked at Jamal through his rearview mirror but didn't say anything else about the situation. He had a feeling his best friend was in some kind of trouble.

They pulled into the garage at Jamal's apartment complex. Maurice drove around a bit until Jamal spotted his car. When Maurice stopped, Jamal got out and shook Maurice's hand.

"Thanks homie," Jamal said.

"No problem. Ay, if you need me for something, you know I got you," Maurice told his friend.

Jamal thought it over. Maurice was a married man now with a baby on the way. There was no way he could get him involved without feeling selfish. He shook his head. "I'm good, Mar. But thanks. Go home and take care of your wife and that baby you got on the way. I'ma holla at you later." He smacked the hood of the car and waited for Maurice to pull away before heading up to his apartment. It then dawned on him that he didn't have Tiffany's breakfast.

The chain was still on the apartment door when he got there. He knocked.

"Marco!" he said to his girlfriend.

"Polo, babe. I'm coming." Tiffany hurried down the hall and unlocked the door for Jamal. He gave her a big hug and kiss.

"Sorry boo, I didn't make it to the diner. It's lunchtime anyway; you want me to order you something?"

"Oh no, it's cool. I was kinda hungry and didn't want to wait so I made some pancakes and sausages for me and Dante. I left you some on the stove in case you didn't eat."

"Thanks babe." He wrapped his arms around her waist and they walked back to the living room where D-Ball was using the laptop.

"You can stop pretending to be handling business on the laptop now, Dante," Tiffany laughed. D-Ball looked up and grinned. "Boy I heard the Facebook notifications go off a couple times. It's cool. But um, the next time you want to send a bodyguard over here, just keep it 100 with me," Tiffany said as she leaned her head back so she could look at Jamal.

Jamal kissed the side of her mouth. "Better safe than sorry. I need to talk to Dante. Can you give us a minute?"

Tiffany nodded and made her way back to their bedroom and closed the door.

"What's up, 'Mal?" D-Ball asked, seeing the serious expression on his friend's face.

"I had a tail earlier. And it wasn't even on some discreet shit at first. I mean they were jumping lights and swerving around Septa buses to keep up with me. I had to dip in the barbershop where my uncle was taken and Skip let me leave out the back so I could cut over to my aunt's house and meet up with my father."

"Are you fucking serious? What the fuck is going on?" D-Ball hissed quietly.

Jamal shook his head. "I would bet money that the niggas who followed me were either the same niggas who took my uncle and Brandon or they were the ones who took the surveillance tapes before we had a chance to get our hands on them."

"Probably. So those niggas coming for you now?" D-Ball asked.

"Hell yeah. And the fucked up thing about it is I found out Lieutenant Jackson, Dennis and get this, my old Lieutenant from D.E is a part of all of this shit."

"Get the fuck outta here?!" D-Ball piped.

Jamal shushed him. "Is that why you had me come sit with Tiff?"

"Yeah 'cause I'll be damned if what happened to Tammy happens to her, too." Jamal said as he glanced at a photo of her on their wall.

"Yeah, shorty's a good look for you. She's definitely a good girl and y'all got a good thing going on. So you gotta hold her down, tough." D-Ball said. "You ain't think to send her somewhere until this shit is over and done with?"

"Yeah, but she reminded me that she's safer with me and not away from me and I agree," Jamal replied as he put his food in the microwave to heat it up.

"I feel you. But this is a crossfire she doesn't want to get caught up in."

"Yeah, I know," Jamal said as he began playing with Tamera's ring that hung from his neck. He twirled it between his fingers before kissing it and letting it fall back to his chest. History was not going to repeat itself. He was willing to put that on his life if need be.

Two days after Jamal met up with his father and gave him the package that Pete was sent to give to him, Andre began carrying out hits like a mad man out of his mind. He started with the easier targets, a sergeant from the Northeast section of Philadelphia being his first target. Andre deactivated his car alarm and waited for him in the back seat before the sergeant came out 5:30 one morning to head to work. When the sergeant sat down and began making adjustments so he could start his day, Andre quietly sat up and put his gun to his head with a silencer connected to the barrel.

"Holy shit!" the sergeant gasped.

"Put your hands on the steering wheel where I can see them. Don't move. Don't talk. You breathe the wrong way and I'ma splatter your muthafucking brains all over this dashboard, capisce?" Andre said in a low and menacing tone. The sergeant swallowed past a knot of fear in his throat and nodded his head as he stared at Andre through his rearview mirror.

ATR 3: The Wrath of Andre

Andre kept his eyes on him along with his gun to his head as he reached for the sergeant's waist and pulled his service revolver. "Ya know, life as a cop can't be too easy. Depressing, if you ask me. You go out every day to risk your life in these streets for these ungrateful people who despise you fucking pigs so much that they wouldn't piss on you if you were on fire. After a while, the pressure just becomes too much to bear, right?" Andre said as he took the sergeant's service revolver and put it to his right temple while holding his own gun to the back of his head.

"Please," the sergeant begged. "Whatever you want, I can give it to you. Just tell me what it is and I'll…"

Andre silenced him by pulling the trigger and blowing a hole in the right side of his head, splattering brain and blood on the driver side window. "Hard head makes a soft behind. I told your muthafucking ass not to talk." He placed the gun in the sergeant's hand and let it lay limp against the arm rest of his car. "Do svidaniya," Andre said before quietly exiting the car; Russian for "Goodbye".

Andre's next target was one of Kristoff's henchmen who helped kill Norman. As bad as Andre wanted to get close to him for a more personal kill, he knew he wouldn't be able to. He decided to try a more indirect approach- a car bomb. Using a non-metallic tap, he was able to put a tail on the henchman when he made a trip down to Maryland to a night-club. Andre waited patiently for his moment to strike. When the perfect opportunity became available, Andre went into the lower level of the parking garage where the car was located. Seeing that the coast was clear, he quickly made his way over to the car and deactivated the alarm just as he did with the sergeant's car. He slid down to the floor of the Ford Five Hundred and quickly and carefully attached the explosive device. He slowly eased out from the seat and closed the car door.

"Do svidaniya," he said as he did a salute to the car and then quickly made his exit.

Inside of the club sat Kristoff, his son, Eli and his henchman, Victor. They were discussing business matters. Eli was tired of playing the background and wanted his father to see him as the man that he had grown to be and realize that he was ready to start conducting big business. Though he was only twenty-four, he had been around the business for quite some time and knew if given a chance, he could make some serious power moves for his father.

"Father, you know that I'm ready. I've been ready. I don't understand why you won't just give me a chance," Eli pestered his father as he refilled his drink of Scotch and soda.

"When the time is right, son. Right now, I have some unfinished business that needs to be taken care of. Once everything is cleared up, then we will discuss the role I intend to have you take on in the business. For now, just keep calm and enjoy the life that I've provided for you," Kristoff said to his son with a grin as a tall beauty came over to the table. She had long dark hair with the body of a Victoria's Secret model. The tall beauty was dressed in a fashionable mini Diane Von Furstenberg dress with six inch heels. She leaned close to Eli putting her arm around him and grinned seductively at him with full, bright red lips. Eli smiled back and let his hand rest on the top of her petite, round backside.

Kristoff reached in his blazer and pulled an envelope from his pocket. "In the meantime, what you can do is take this back to the hotel suite and put it in the safe. I meant to do it earlier but I was a little preoccupied with business.”

Eli shook his head and grabbed the envelope from his father. “This errand boy shit…”

“Hey, watch your tongue, son.” Kristoff warned with fire in his eyes.

Eli did his best to keep the next sarcastic response from falling from his mouth. He tucked the envelope in his inner jacket pocket. “I take it Victor will be playing babysitter again?”

Kristoff snapped his fingers in his son’s direction. “Victor, take him and bring him back here afterwards,” he instructed.

Victor nodded his head as he stood up. Eli made his way out of the booth that they were all sitting in and Victor followed behind. Once they were down in the garage, Eli turned to Victor.

“Can I at least drive or does dear old dad expect me to play the background in the car too?” Eli asked sarcastically.

Victor tossed him the keys, “It’s okay with me.”

“I’ll be so glad when dad stops treating me like some little bitch that doesn’t know shit. I’m just as capable of getting things done as he is," Eli said as they made their way over to the car.

"It's not that your father doesn't think you're capable, Eli, he just has some heat that he wants to take care of before he can just hand the reins over to you. A real man doesn't pass his problems down to his son." Victor explained.

"Yeah, I guess so," Eli sulked. They both climbed into the car. "I just can't wait for the day when dad lets me handle things so I can show him I can really blow this business up." Eli stuck the key in the ignition and turned it. The starter triggered the explosive device that Andre set in the car and the car exploded, partially lifting from the ground. It rocked back and forth as the scorching flames quickly charred and burned the vehicle along with its occupants.

Andre watched from a safe distance as he smoked a cigarette. "Two for the price of one. Do svidaniya, muthafuckas." He flicked his cigarette and got into his car, pulling off before first responders came onto the scene.

15

Jamal's mother was being discharged from the hospital but needed to go to rehab. Shawn and Jamal agreed that it would be best if she came to Italy to stay with him to do her rehab which would keep her off the radar in the event she was targeted again.

"Damn shame I had to get shot to make it out of this God forsaken country," Keyona said as Jamal wheeled her out of the hospital and over to his car where Tiffany was waiting for them. "We all have something in common now, Jamal."

Jamal laughed, knowing what she was talking about. "How about that, mom?"

Tiffany smiled when they got closer to her and Keyona smiled back.

"We finally meet," Keyona said, extending her hand to Tiffany for a handshake.

"Nice to meet you, Mrs. Williams," Tiffany spoke politely with a smile.

"Nice to meet you, too. Jamal done went and got himself a pretty little chocolate girl. She is gorgeous, boy." Keyona squealed. Jamal chuckled and helped his mother from the wheelchair and into the car before fastening her in.

"Thanks mom." He closed her door and he and Tiffany got in the front to take Keyona straight to the airport to catch her flight. Keyona smiled at the way the two of them held hands while Jamal drove. She could tell that her son was in love with this new young lady and she was happy for him. She had not seen her son this happy since he was with Tamera more than ten years prior.

After Keyona made it past the metal detectors, Jamal flashed his badge. The security guards nodded at him and let both he and Tiffany by without going through the metal detectors.

"Damn," Tiffany whispered. "Being a detective has its perks." Jamal chuckled as he pushed his mother over to the boarding area.

He knelt in front of her. "Mom, I got you a new phone. Check in with me when you land. It's a straight flight so you don't have to worry about a layover. Chanda and the kids are going to be waiting for you when you land. I think Shawn is at an away game in Germany but will be back in a couple of days."

"Okay," Keyona said with a smile. "As long as they take me to the Coliseum, I'm good." Jamal hugged her tightly but frowned when he heard his mother wince and felt her tighten up in his arms.

"Sorry, ma," he apologized as he let her go. "Have a safe flight."

"I will," she waved to her son and his girlfriend as an attendee came to wheel her onto the plane. Jamal watched until she disappeared down the corridor. Tiffany could tell that he was worried so she grabbed his hand and intertwined their fingers.

"I still think you should go to New York," Jamal said as he looked down at her.

Tiffany shook her head, "No, Jamal. I'm not leaving you."

Jamal stared down at her for a moment and shook his head at her defiance. He put his arm around her and they walked back to his car. They talked during the drive home as they listened to music. His personal phone was going off with calls from Pete and D-Ball but he was unable to hear it because it was on vibrate. Moments after he pulled up to his apartment complex, four marked cars pulled up also. Jamal looked around at them, puzzled.

"Detective Williams?" one of the officers said to him as he got out of the car.

"Yeah?" Jamal replied, not having a good feeling.

"We need you to come with us," the officer said.

"What the fuck for?" Jamal asked with hostility.

One of the officers grabbed him and pushed him up against the car.

"What the hell are you doing?" Tiffany asked feeling frightened. Her heart raced as she watched the officers search Jamal and take both of his guns. They then pulled his hands behind his back and slapped handcuffs on him.

"Jamal Williams, you're under arrest for obstruction of justice. You have the right to remain silent…"

"This is bullshit," Jamal said as he shook his head.

"Is that even necessary?" Tiffany practically screamed as she tried to follow behind the officer that was walking Jamal to the squad car.

"Ma'am, we're going to have to ask you to step back," another officer said as he put a hand in front of Tiffany to stop her.

"Anything you say can be used against you in a court of law. You have the right to an attorney. If you cannot afford an attorney, one will be appointed to you by the state."

"Man, what the fuck ever," Jamal snapped as they opened the car door.

"Jamal, what do you want me to do?" Tiffany asked as her eyes became teary.

"Just call Dante and tell him to come to the apartment. Get his number from my cell phone in the car," Jamal instructed her. He was placed inside of the squad car and the officers got in and pulled off one by one.

Tiffany hurried back to the car to get the cell phone. She saw it but then heard another one ring. She flicked the light on so she could see and saw his other phone that she wasn't familiar with. She frowned as she picked it up wondering if she should answer it.

"Hello…?" she said tentatively.

Andre paused. "Who is this?"

"You called my boyfriend's phone. Who the hell are you?" Tiffany replied instantly in a shitty mood after seeing Jamal handcuffed and taken away like some common criminal and then discovering he had a second phone that she knew nothing about.

"Tiffany," Andre said in a matter of fact manner. "Where's Jamal?"

"How do you know my name?"

"Never mind that. Where is Jamal?"

"The cops just handcuffed him and took him away," Tiffany explained trying to keep her composure.

"What the fuck for?" Andre piped, as he stood up.

"Obstruction of justice or something like that. Who are you?" Tiffany asked again.

"Are you home?" Andre asked.

Not knowing who the man was on the other phone, Tiffany disconnected the call. She snatched up Jamal's other phone and called D-Ball as she headed up to their apartment.

"Yo!" D-Ball answered, thinking it was Jamal.

"Dante! It's Tiff. They just handcuffed Jamal and took him away," Tiffany said hastily as she unlocked the apartment door and went inside. She locked all of the locks and set the alarm.

"For what?" D-Ball replied as he stopped at a red light.

"Obstruction of justice. Jamal told me to call you and ask you to come over until this is sorted out. Will you be able to?" Tiffany asked as she scrolled through Jamal's second phone. She saw that it was only the one number that the man called from, no text messages or anything else and became even more confused.

"Yeah, I'm on my way. Sit tight; don't open the door for nobody. I'm not even gonna knock, I'ma just call you when I get to the door, okay?" D-Ball said to her as he sped off when the light changed to green.

"Okay." Tiffany disconnected the phone and paced the living room. Jamal had a second phone with only one number in it that went to a man who seemed to know Jamal, though she never heard of or met him. *"Why would Jamal need a second phone just to talk to that one person?"* she wondered to herself. She went to their bedroom and began looking around. She searched the top of the closet and inside of shoe boxes. She then looked on the shelves inside of their walk-in closet and underneath a stack of paper she found a manila envelope. She peeked inside and pulled a few of the papers out, immediately being able to see that they were police documents. She sat on the edge of the bed and pulled all of the papers out and began scanning them. Tiffany became very intrigued when she saw the documents were about Samir Muhammad's murder investigation.

"Andre Williams?" Tiffany mumbled as she read. She thumbed through the papers until she came across some photos. She looked at the same one that caught Jamal's attention months before and frowned. To make sure her eyes weren't deceiving her, she reached onto the night table for her eye glasses and put them on. She looked at the photo again and then thought back to the day she decided to take the stairs to the apartment because the lights had gone out and bumped into the man coming through the doors that led to the stairway. The man who she told Jamal looked just like him. Her heart raced as she shook her head and looked at the photo again. "Is this your father?" she asked out loud.

She heard a knock at the door and jumped. She trembled as she put the papers back in the envelope and placed them back in the closet the way she found them.

"Who is it?" she asked.

"Police ma'am, we need to speak with you, please?" she heard a man's voice say.

Tiffany hesitated. Why would the police want to talk to her? She tip-toed over to the door and looked through the peep-hole. She could see that there were two uniformed officers but one was partially out of her vision and the other had his head down slightly so she could not see his face. She un-locked the top lock and the lock on the door knob but left the chain-lock attached and opened it just enough to see out. Before she could say anything, one of the men pushed forcefully on the door, snapping the chain and Tiffany screamed, jumping back. The men barged into her home and she backed away down the hallway. She looked at the both of them frightened. When the first one lunged for her, she grabbed an African Barbie-sized statue from a table in the hallway and swung with it, catching the first officer in the face with it. The hit cut open the side of his face and blood streamed out. He staggered back in shock and in pain.

"Bitch!" the second one said as he came for her.

Tiffany swung again but the officer dodged her attempt and grabbed her by the wrist, bending it back to make her drop it. She hollered out in pain but grabbed the man by his collar with her other hand and kicked him on the side of his knee hoping to dislocate it. He buckled, letting her wrist go and Tiffany used her palm to hit him in the nose, busting it and making him fall back. She turned to run but the first officer lunged for her making her fall to the floor. They struggled with each other back and forth, knocking over knick-knacks and photo frames from the table until the officer grabbed for her throat and began to squeeze. She gagged and clawed at his hands trying to get him off but to no avail. Her feet peddled until she was able to raise her knees and she kneed the officer in the groin twice. When his grip loosened, she scooted away from him enough to get her feet up and kicked him in his chest, knocking him back. She was dizzy and struggling to breathe after her airway was cut off but tried to crawl to the bedroom to get her gun. She heard gunshots from behind her and opened her mouth to scream but couldn't get a sound out.

"Tiff!" D-Ball hollered out.

Tiffany turned over and looked at him breathing heavy and in tears. He extended his hand to her and helped her up. She struggled to catch her breath as she let his hand go and went to their bedroom. She grabbed her gun, Jamal's two cell-phones and then grabbed the manila envelope and stumbled back to D-Ball handing it to him.

"Come on, we gotta get the hell outta here," D-Ball said.

Tiffany closed the door and they were about to hurry down the hall when they saw two men coming in their direction. Without hesitation, one aimed at them and fired. D-Ball pushed Tiffany back after they both ducked.

"Pussy!" D-Ball growled as he fired back rapidly, hitting one of them. The other man jumped back. "Run, Tiff! Move!" D-Ball yelled. They turned to run and burst through the doors to go down the stairs but saw two men coming up. D-Ball snatched Tiffany back making her stumble out of her shoe. She took her other shoe off and they ran upstairs instead. They burst through the doors to the seventh floor and hauled assed down the hallway. Just as they were turning the corner, someone behind them fired shots at them.

ATR 3: The Wrath of Andre

"Shit!" D-Ball screamed. He grabbed Tiffany by the arm and they ran down another hallway until they saw a door leading to an outside balcony. D-Ball kicked it in and they ran out, skipping steps to get down the fire escape. They were almost to the bottom when someone fired at them from above. D-Ball pushed Tiffany down and fired back at them. He heard someone yelp, letting him know he hit them and then he and Tiffany continued running until they hit the pavement. Bystanders screamed and ducked out of the way as D-Ball turned to shoot at the fire escape to give them some lead way and then he and Tiffany ran down the street. Tiffany was getting ready to make a left turn to the garage to get Jamal's car, but D-Ball snatched her by the arm and made her go right instead to his car. They jumped inside and sped off.

Tiffany was hyperventilating, unable to get her breathing fully under control after being choked and then running for her life. D-Ball could hear her whimpering as she wheezed terribly.

"Breathe Tiff, it's okay. Take a slow breath. Relax, we're good now. We're good," D-Ball tried to reassure her as he sped down the street.

Tiffany let out a dry cough and then puked on the floor of his car.

"Ahh fuck!" D-Ball said. "I just cleaned this shit," he shook his head.

Finally able to get her breathing under control, she burst out in tears. "I'm sorry!"

"It's cool. Are you okay? Are you bleeding, did you get hit?" D-Ball asked as he sped through a yellow light.

Tiffany took trembling breaths and shook her head. "No…what the hell is going on?!" she asked D-Ball frantically.

Before D-Ball could answer, his back window was shot out. Tiffany screamed and ducked. D-Ball ducked as well, swerving the car.

"Yo! These muthafuckas are not playing!" D-Ball yelled as he made a sharp left turn and sped down a street. He looked back quickly and saw a silver Lesabre make a speedy turn right behind them. "Tiff, I know you're scared, but I need you to bust back. I know Jamal taught you how to shoot and I know you got your burner on you, I saw when you grabbed it…"

D-Ball was cut off by the sound of more bullets hitting the back of his car.

"Shit! Shoot back! Shoot back!" D-Ball yelled at Tiffany.

ATR 3: The Wrath of Andre

Tiffany grabbed her gun and positioned herself between her seat and D-Ball's seat. She aimed out of the back window that had been shot out and squeezed her trigger. She hit the windshield, aiming for head shots and the car chasing them swerved.

"Yeah! That's right, Tiff! Fuck them niggas up!" D-Ball exclaimed as he honked his horn to make pedestrians get out of his way. He swerved around a right corner almost jumping the curb and decided to head over to the police station hoping that would be of some help.

"I'm out!" Tiff yelled.

"Oh hell no!" D-Ball said. He steered the car with his left hand and pulled his glock 9 from his waist before handing it to Tiffany.

"I never shot with a glock before," Tiffany said.

"Well, you gon' learn today. Aim with both of your hands," D-Ball instructed her as he made an illegal left turn onto Broad Street. "Hold on!" he told her as he quickly jumped in front of another car, cutting them off and making them swerve. Cars honked at him but D-Ball didn't give a shit. He was trying to get the hell away from the car chasing him. At the intersection of Lindley and Broad Street, the light was turning red. D-Ball shook his head and pressed down on the accelerator. He timed it just right to swerve around the back of one car coming through the intersection. Cars swerved behind him. He hoped he could cause a crash with the car chasing him, but they managed to dodge the swerving cars.

"Come the fuck on man!" D-Ball said. He cut another car off to speed around a Septa bus. The car chasing them stayed with them. "Any other time, when I need the fucking lights on Broad Street to stay green, the muthafuckas are all red. Now today, I want the muthafuckas to be red and the muthafucking lights are all green!" D-Ball ranted as he dipped from one lane to another. He saw a double Septa bus ahead in the middle lane and jumped in the far right lane. Tiffany saw what he intended to do.

"Oh my God!" she squealed as she grabbed the back of the head rest.

D-Ball saw that the light was about to turn green ahead and the bus changed to the far right lane to make a right turn. D-Ball swerved back to the middle lane and gunned it so he could catch up to the bus and then made a quick right turn in front of it before the light turned green. The car behind them tried to make the same turn as the bus was pulling off and the bus smashed right into it.

"Yeah!" D-Ball exclaimed, as he banged his fist on the steering wheel. "Take that shit, muthafuckas! We out! Ha ha!"

Tiffany looked out the back window at the accident behind them and then faced forward. She placed her hand to her chest and closed her eyes. She was beginning to wish she had taken her ass to New York after all.

Jamal's second phone went off. Tiffany answered it quickly. "I know who you are…Andre."

D-Ball looked at Tiffany wide-eyed but then turned his attention back to the road. Instead of driving to the police station, he decided to go back to his old neighborhood. He still had some goons that were ready to ride for him if need be.

"Where are you?" Andre asked.

"Someone just tried to kill me in me and Jamal's apartment. Thankfully his partner showed up. We barely made it out of there alive," Tiffany explained.

"I know. There's cops all over at your place. Where are you, now?" Andre asked again.

"I'm with Dante…uh D-Ball; Jamal's partner." Tiffany looked out the window. "We're coming up Cecil B. Moore Avenue near 17th Street."

"Put D-Ball on the phone," Andre instructed.

Tiffany handed the phone to D-Ball."

"Yo!" D-Ball said into the handset.

"You know who this is?" Andre asked.

"Of course, it's the legendary Andre Williams, back from the dead. We need to start calling you "Death" because it seems like that's all you're bringing with you," D-Ball said in a half joking manner.

"Switch cars. I'm going to text you the address to where you need to come. Get here in one hour." Andre disconnected the call. D-Ball looked at the phone briefly and then drove over to his friend's garage off of 29th and Girard.

"I'm out here with no shoes on," Tiffany frowned as she got out the car.

"Hey, it could be worse. Your ass could be dead," D-Ball said as he walked over to the garage. "Stay right here." He whistled for his friend the mechanic to come up from under the hood of a Ford Explorer that he was working on.

ATR 3: The Wrath of Andre

"D-Ball! What's popping, my man?" the mechanic said as he wiped his hands on a rag and then shook D-Ball's hand.

"Listen, I ran into some trouble a while back. I can't really get into it. I need to hold one of your whips real quick." The mechanic came out and looked Tiffany over. He looked down at her feet and saw she didn't have any shoes on. He then looked at D-Ball's car and walked around the back of it. When he saw the windshield was shot out and there were bullet holes in the bumper and trunk, he whistled and shook his head.

"Damn, homie. Not the CTS," he said as he shook his head again.

"Yeah man, shit just got real. You got something I can hold for a bit?" D-Ball asked. He reached in his back pocket and pulled out a knot of money and peeled off four one hundred dollar bills. "I need you to fix this for me."

"Man, you know we go back like hi-top Reeboks and ankle socks. I got you, homie." The mechanic slapped D-Ball a handshake. "Sweetheart, what size shoes do you wear? About a seven?" the mechanic asked Tiffany.

She looked down at her feet feeling embarrassed that she wasn't wearing shoes. "Yes," she replied.

"Ay yo, Bob! Reach in that bag and bring out those Jordan's back there." Bob brought him the Jordan's as asked and the mechanic handed them to Tiffany. "I just bought these for my son. He's a six which should be an eight in women. A little too big but it beats walking around with nothing on your feet. You're too pretty for that."

"Oh wow, thank you!" Tiffany smiled. "I can come back and pay you for them…"

The mechanic waved her off, "Don't worry about it," he told her with a charismatic smile.

"That's 'Mal's girl, Rick. Don't even think about it." D-Ball said as he stood close to him while Tiffany put the sneakers on. She looked them over and smiled.

"She bad as shit," the mechanic mumbled back to D-Ball. "'Mal stay pulling all the bad jawns."

D-Ball laughed, "Yo, you wild! Let me get a whip real quick. I gotta get outta here."

"Only if I get to drive this bitch when I finish replacing that window. I can have that fixed by the end of the day. It's going to take a minute to get a bumper to replace this one."

"Alright, I'll swap with you for now. But don't be using my shit to pick up no chicks, Rick," D-Ball warned as Rick tossed him a set of keys.

"Man, please. You need to come around more often. I don't need this to pick up bitches when I got that." Rick pointed to the shiny black 2012 Range Rover.

D-Ball put his fist to his mouth. "Okay, my nigga! You out here stunting on these niggas!" They slapped each other a handshake. "I'ma holla at you."

"Yeah, just don't get my shit all shot the fuck up while you out there. You cool, nigga? You got heat?" Rick asked.

"Nah, nothing I can't handle. You know how I roll." D-Ball lifted his shirt up to show he had both his glock 9 and Desert Eagle.

Rick lifted his shirt up in return to expose his .357 Magnum. "You ain't said nothing but a word. Just call me Dirty Harry out this bitch." They both laughed again before D-Ball hopped in the Range Rover and sped off. Tiffany looked at the phone and saw the text message that Andre sent letting them know where to go. She read the directions to D-Ball and they headed over there.

17

Jamal sat in the back of the police car handcuffed. He didn't bother making any conversation with the officers who arrested him, making sure he exercised his right to remain silent. He thought back to when they said he was under arrest for obstruction of justice. More than likely this was their way of putting pressure on him to tell them who else was in his mother's house the night that she was shot. He had already made up his mind; he wasn't telling them shit.

He looked out of the window and saw that they were no where near the police station on Broad Street and Old York Road. Where the hell were they taking him?

"Umm, you niggas lost or something? Y'all ain't no where near the station," Jamal said to them. When they didn't respond, Jamal looked behind him and didn't see the other units following anymore. He looked around to see where they were and began to get a bad feeling. "Where the fuck are y'all taking me?" Jamal asked. He still received no answer. He twisted his hands against the cuffs and cursed under his breath. He had no burner, no phone, nothing to help him get out of this shit. His thoughts began to wander back to what Pete told him that he heard between Lieutenant Jackson and Dennis. They cooked up a bullshit arrest to get him away from Tiffany. He prayed like shit that D-Ball got to her in time and she was okay. If something had been done to her, no amount of rationalization would keep him from murdering everything in his path.

He told himself to remain calm and not to panic. Panic would only make his situation worse. He took a deep breath and closed his eyes, thinking of his mother, his brother and his girlfriend. He then thought of his uncle and imagined he experienced something similar. When the car stopped, Jamal opened his eyes and looked around. He was at what resembled a warehouse. The officers had taken him to the same place that Norman and Brandon had been taken to.

They opened the car door and pulled Jamal out. He didn't resist, he kept his cool and walked where they led him, down to the same basement that

Norman fought and died in. The cops stood on both sides of Jamal while they waited for instructions. Jamal looked around to get an idea of his surroundings, a possible escape route if given the opportunity as well as if there was anything in there that could be used as a weapon.

After a few minutes, Kristoff made his appearance. His hair was still a mixture of grey and black- the salt and pepper look, with his mustache and beard being a jet black color to match his eyes, which were even colder than before. His only son had been murdered in the car explosion that Andre orchestrated and he was done playing Mr. Nice Guy.

"Take his handcuffs off. He's no threat to me," Kristoff said to the two officers as he looked Jamal in the eyes. It was the first time he had seen him up close and personal. The fact that he resembled Andre so much made him want to plunge a knife in his abdomen and watch him die slowly in front of him. But it wouldn't satisfy his desire to kill Andre. Nothing would beat killing the real thing.

Kristoff stared at Jamal for a long time as he twirled the cross around his neck. When the handcuffs were off, Jamal rubbed his wrists and rotated his hands to shake off the pain from the cuffs being so tight on him. He stared back wondering if he was finally face to face with Kristoff.

Kristoff fixed his eyes on the ring that Jamal wore around his neck and then looked Jamal in his eyes before saying anything. Finally, he leaned on the metal table and cleared his throat. "You know who I am?" he asked Jamal.

"Am I supposed to?" Jamal asked back.

Kristoff didn't smile. He continued to stare at Jamal and Jamal stared back not feeling intimidated in the slightest. "You should know who I am. My name is Alekzander Kristoff. I'm sure you are familiar with that name."

"Yeah…so?" Jamal replied flatly. Kristoff looked at the ring around Jamal's neck again.

"You know, you and I are quite similar," Kristoff started as he began to pace while twirling the cross that hung from his neck between his fingers.

"I doubt it," Jamal said as he followed Kristoff with his eyes.

"Oh trust me. We are. The ring you wear around your neck is in memory of a love long lost. You wear it as though it will protect you, guide you, keep you and never forsake you. You wear it to remind yourself of what was lost and to make sure any miscalculation you made before is never made again to avoid suffering that kind of lost once more."

Jamal sighed, "Get to the fucking point. Don't talk like you know me. You don't know shit about me."

Kristoff looked at Jamal sharply as he stopped pacing. "This cross was my wife's. Many years ago she wore it every single day. Never took it off. When she got down on her knees to pray in the morning and at night, she would finish her prayer off by kissing it. She was taken from me, similar to the way your Tamera was taken from you. I keep this cross as my way of keeping her with me just as you keep Tamera's ring as a way of keeping her with you." Kristoff fell silent as he leaned back on the metal table. Jamal watched him as he kissed the cross and let it fall back to his chest and it reminded him of the many times he did the same thing with Tamera's ring.

"I'm still waiting for you to get to the fucking point. I know damn well you didn't bring me all the way down here to compare notes on how we choose to honor the dead. What the fuck do you want?"

"Your lack of respect and insolence is enough for me to kill your nigger-ass right here, right now," Kristoff said with malice.

Yani

"The fuck did you just call me?" Jamal asked with a raised eye-brow.

Kristoff smiled. "You heard me. Your father murdered my son and outside of killing that Black bastard with my bare hands, killing you is the next best thing that seems satisfactory."

"And your bitch-ass killed my uncle and my cousin and sent your nut-ass goons after my mom. If you're going to kill me muthafucka you better make sure you get it done right because I promise you won't get a second chance," Jamal said in a voice so cold it almost made Kristoff recoil. Kristoff smiled at Jamal. He had a feeling he was going to be the challenge that he needed.   "Where's Andre, Jamal?" Kristoff asked coolly just as he did when he asked Norman.

Jamal shrugged. "How the fuck am I supposed to know? But give him some time, you'll see him soon. I'm sure you're on his to kill list." Jamal smirked.

Kristoff stared at him for a moment and then waved at the officer that was still standing in the doorway. The officer left and then returned moments later with a beaten and bruised Pete. The officer pushed him into the room and he stumbled, almost falling. Jamal winced when he saw him. He extended a hand to help him stand up.

"Pete…" Jamal said, feeling bad for his friend.

Pete looked at him frightened and then looked at Kristoff.

"How many of your friends and family members do I have to kill before you give me what I fucking want? It's really very simple."

"Fuck you," Jamal said spitefully.

Kristoff wagged his finger as if chastising a dog. "Tsk, tsk, tsk, Jamal." Kristoff nodded at the officer behind them. Before Jamal or Pete had a chance to brace themselves, the officer came behind Pete and put a sharp knife in his back. Pete arched his back frowning in pain as blood spilled from his mouth. The cop took the blade out and jabbed it in his back again, going deeper. Jamal looked at them in horror as Pete grabbed onto him before sliding to the floor. Jamal looked down at Pete breathing heavy and then looked at Kristoff, seeing him as the evil bastard he was.

"Consider that a warning. And it's the only warning I'm giving you. His blood is on your hands. I want Andre. And I fucking want him tonight or what

I did to Norman will seem like fucking cake compared to what I'll do to you," Kristoff warned. He then smiled a smile filled with malice and evil. "Norman fought his ass off to the end. I wonder will you last as long."

Jamal lunged for Kristoff, gripping him by his collar. The chain that he wore around his neck was caught in his grasped and popped off when Jamal let him go with one hand and punched him in his jaw making him stagger back. He was about to swing again when the officer that stabbed Pete grabbed Jamal and put him in a choke hold with one of his arms behind his back. Jamal struggled against him.

"You little mother fucker," Kristoff said as he picked his broken chain up from off of the floor. He tossed it lightly in his hand before stuffing it in his pocket and then hauled off and back slapped Jamal, cutting him on the side of his face with the ring he wore. He then hit Jamal twice in the ribs, partially making him buckle. The officer pushed Jamal to the floor. "You've got one hour to give up your father or you'll lose a finger like Norman. Maybe even more," Kristoff threatened before leaving the room and slamming and locking the door behind him.

ATR 3: The Wrath of Andre

Jamal sat up and wiped the blood from the side of his face. His ribs were a little sore but he ignored his pain as he turned his attention to Pete. He noticed the glasses were hanging from his shirt as they were the day he came to his apartment and a glimmer of hope came alive within him. He looked at the door to make sure there was no little window for someone outside to look in and see what he was about to do. When he saw that it wasn't, he crawled over to Pete and pretended to try to revive him, though he knew his friend was already dead.

"I'm so sorry, Pete. I never meant for this to happen." He turned Pete onto his back and looked at the glasses. "Dad, if you can see this, I need your help. Please. Dad, I need you, please come help me." Jamal sat back and looked around. He prayed that his dad came to help him within the next hour. He wasn't ready to die.

18

D-Ball pulled up to where Andre told him to go. It was a small house in Chestnut Hill that sat by itself. He and Tiffany walked up to the door and were about to knock when Andre opened it for them. He motioned for them to come in quickly. D-Ball and Tiffany looked around with their mouths partially hanging open. It looked like a CIA operation in there. Andre had views on multiple monitors. There was video surveillance of Jamal's apartment, Denise's house and Keyona's house. There was also the video surveillance from Pete's glasses where Andre had just seen him take a severe beating. He was standing by a table loading up guns with bullets. He had regular, hollow tip and armor piercing bullets. D-Ball was astonished at the different caliber of guns Andre had.

"Yo, you about to be my muthafucking hero!" D-Ball said excitedly as he picked up an M-80 grenade. Andre smirked as he slammed a clip into a 9MM and sat it on the table.

"Did either of you call the station about Jamal?" Andre asked as he looked at them. He fixed his eyes on Tiffany and smiled. Tiffany looked away feeling uncomfortable after seeing there was surveillance in their apartment. She was wondering how much Andre had seen.

Andre sensed that was what she was thinking and said, "Don't worry, I don't have surveillance in the bedroom. Just the hallway, living room and dining room. You handled yourself very well earlier. I can see why my son is so into you," Andre smiled.

Tiffany let out a sigh of relief. "Thank you."

"I didn't get a chance to call the station because of all the shit that went down when I got to their apartment. But I can call right now. Tiff said he was arrested for obstruction…"

Andre put up a hand to silence D-Ball. "Don't bother, he's not there," he said. "I called and told them I was his best friend, Maurice, and wanted to see if bail was necessary to get him out or if he was just being questioned. He was never brought in."

"Are you sure you called the right station?" Tiffany asked as her heart raced.

Andre nodded his head. "They didn't even have a record of an arrest warrant for Jamal."

"Sonuva bitch!" D-Ball said as he shook his head. Tiffany put her hands to her mouth as she looked at Andre.

"So now what?" she asked.

D-Ball pointed to the screen that displayed the surveillance from the glasses Pete had on his shirt. They could see Jamal in view. "Look!"

They all fixed their eyes on the screen and watched as things unfolded. When Pete was stabbed, the look on Jamal's face let them know that something deathly was wrong. Tiffany turned away from the screen when she saw Jamal being put in a choke hold.

Andre went over to a computer screen and pulled up Pete's surveillance. He rewound it back to when he was first taken and enhanced the image to get a view of what was outside. He took a screen shot of the front of the building Pete was being walked to and put the image in Google Search. Moments later the address came up. It wasn't too far from them.

"Time to roll," Andre said as he grabbed a duffle bag. He tossed a bullet proof vest to D-Ball and one to Tiffany. She looked at it confused. "You're coming too, Little Lady.

"You sure about that?" D-Ball asked as he quickly took his shirt off and put his vest on."

"Tiff, do you want to sit on the sideline filled with worry, or do you want to stand by your man?" Andre asked as he put on a vest and handed a gun and two clips to D-Ball. D-Ball checked them out of habit and then put the gun in the small of his back.

Tiffany thought over what Andre said and then pulled her shirt over her head so she could put her vest on as well. D-Ball helped her fasten it and Andre handed her a 9MM.

"Did Jamal teach you how to shoot with that?" D-Ball asked her.

"Yeah, it was the first one we practiced with." She then remembered what Jamal always told her and she said it out loud. "Shoot to kill, not to injure, because the other person may not give you the same courtesy."

"Bingo," Andre said as he threw the M-80s in the duffle bag and walked to the door. "This is straight kill or be killed. Keep your head down and your gun drawn. We're going in to get my boy. If you get an opportunity to take out Kristoff, don't fucking hesitate. Let's move."

They left out of the house. Tiffany kept the gun in her hand but held it underneath her shirt in case anyone was outside, they would not be able to see it. D-Ball and Tiffany jumped in the black Range Rover and Andre jumped inside of a black Chevy Silverado. He revved the engine up and sped off with D-Ball quickly following behind.

"You ready for this?" D-Ball asked Tiffany after glancing at her and seeing her eyes were closed and her mouth was moving. He could tell she was praying.

She nodded her head at first but then shook it. "No, I'm not. But I can't let anything happen to him. I love him and I can't see myself without him."

D-Ball smiled. "Stay with me in there. Cover my back and I'll cover yours. I get the feeling "Death" won't need us to cover him."

"Death?" Tiffany repeated as she looked at D-Ball.

"Yeah…Andre. That's what I'm calling that nigga from now on if we make it out of this shit alive."

Andre drove slowly past the location where Jamal was to get an idea of what the front was like. He saw that two guys were standing out front smoking a cigarette and talking. Neither of them were paying him any mind. D-Ball looked at them and continued following behind Andre. He circled around back to get an idea of what it looked like back there as well and saw there was a side entrance. He remembered from the video that Pete was taken down a flight of stairs so he was positive Jamal was in the basement. He sped up to make sure he didn't draw attention and parked a half of a block away. D-Ball pulled up right behind him and he and Tiffany got out of the car. They walked over to him and awaited his instructions.

"So what's the plan…Death?" D-Ball asked with a half-smile on his face.

Andre smiled at the nick-name D-Ball had given him and then held up the device he used to cause black outs. "We're going around the side. I have a silencer so if there is a chain-lock, I'm shooting it off. Anybody between us and the basement where Jamal is gets popped no questions asked. I'm the only one with a silencer so don't shoot unless you absolutely have to. Once it's clear, wait for my signal," Andre instructed.

"What's the signal?" Tiffany asked.

"Complete darkness," Andre replied as he got out of the truck.

"How do you know Jamal is in the basement? What if he's somewhere else?" Tiffany asked, feeling nervous.

"Because it's always the basement," D-Ball replied.

Andre looked Tiffany over. He reached in his pocket and handed her a stick of gum. "Now ain't the time to be nervous, Little Lady. Nervousness will get you killed in there. Get it together," Andre said firmly.

Tiffany put the chewing gum in her mouth and nodded. They hurried over to the side door with Andre taking point and D-Ball and Tiffany behind him.

"Stay close to me," D-Ball said to Tiffany again.

"I will," Tiffany replied as she nodded her head.

Andre gently pushed on the side door not surprised to see the thick rope chain preventing it from being opened fully. He held it open with his foot and then aimed at the chain before shooting it until it broke apart. He grabbed the pieces and quietly pulled on them until he was able to get the door open. When he did, Andre held his hand up for D-Ball and Tiffany to wait before entering. D-Ball checked behind them to make sure no one was coming. Andre didn't see anyone on either end of the long hallway and signaled D-Ball and Tiffany to follow behind him.

"Wait right here," he said to them in a low voice. He reached in his duffle bag and handed three M-80s to D-Ball. "Use these shits wisely." He ducked down low and crept down to one end of the hallway. He peeked around the corner and saw one of Kristoff's men leaned against the wall twirling keys around his finger. Andre aimed for a head shot and squeezed the trigger, catching the unsuspecting victim in the side of the head. The guy slid to the floor with a thud. Andre looked on to see if anyone would come. When no one did, he crept over to the guy and took the keys from him. He eased down the hall and saw a wide opened room with three guys inside but Kristoff wasn't one of them. Andre hooked the keys to his belt buckle and used his trigger to cut the lights.

Tiffany jumped when the lights went off. D-Ball tapped her.

"Game time," he said to her as he pulled his second gun and started heading down the other end of the hallway. The lighting was mediocre and Tiffany was glad that she chose to wear dark colors that day seeing that it would help her to blend in with the shadows. They could hear guys chattering about what happened to the lights. D-Ball peeped around the corner to see how many of them were there and quickly counted five of them. Just as he thought to use one of the M-80s that Andre gave to him, they heard an explosion from the side where Andre had gone. They both ducked down. D-Ball took one of the M-80s and threw it in the direction where the five guys were at knowing that they would be headed their way to check out what was going on. The M-80 exploded and they heard screams filled with surprise, horror and pain.

"Get down," D-Ball told Tiffany. She crouched down and aimed in the direction D-Ball aimed in. D-Ball slid out aiming one gun in the direction he threw the M-80 in while aiming his other gun in the direction that Andre went. Tiffany had a hunch to look behind them and saw someone coming. She aimed at them and fired twice putting them down. She heard gunshots coming from where Andre went and was turned back around when she heard the loud boom from D-Ball's Desert Eagle. D-Ball was a skilled two-gun shooter with a quick aim.

He fired quickly at a few of the guys who weren't killed in the M-80 explosion. Tiffany stood up and stayed at his back watching the other end of the hallway with her gun drawn. When D-Ball ran out of bullets with one gun, she returned fire to give him a chance to reload. They made their way down the smoke-filled hallway past the men they had just put down. The sprinklers came on to extinguish the fire that erupted from the M-80s D-Ball and Andre threw. A guy came up behind Tiffany and grabbed her making her drop her gun. She reached behind her and grabbed the back of his head and then stomped his foot. She was able to hook her arm around the back of his neck as he tried to wrap his arms around her waist and she elbowed him in the ribs. When he bent over in pain, she yanked away from him and elbowed him in his temple before kicking him in his stomach and put him down. Out the corner of her eye she saw another guy aim a gun at her and she dove to the floor in the direction of her gun. The water on the floor from the sprinklers caused her to slide but she was able to grab her gun. She turned on her side and quickly fired at the guy aiming at her, shooting him twice in the stomach and put him down. She wasn't sure if he was dead so she got up and kicked his gun away from him.

D-Ball saw how she was able to handle herself and grinned.

"Come on," he told her as they made their way down another hallway.

Tiffany searched wildly from left to right to see if anyone was coming, occasionally checking behind her. She saw someone come from out of a room and quickly aimed at him, shooting him twice in the chest and once in the stomach.

"Damn girl!" D-Ball said as he looked back at her.

Tiffany didn't say anything, not wanting to be distracted. A door opened on their right and Tiffany turned to fire at him but was out of bullets. "Fuck!" she exclaimed. The guy smiled at her but she threw her gun at him, catching him in the throat. When he reached for his neck out of reflex, Tiffany ducked and D-Ball fired at him, hitting him in the head. The guy fell back and then slumped to the floor.

"Keep a count of the bullets you fire!" D-Ball scolded her.

"I'm sorry!" Tiffany said back as she dumped her clip and put a fresh one in. She chambered a round and followed behind D-Ball.

He turned the corner too quickly and didn't have enough time to respond. One of the uniformed cops shot D-Ball twice putting him down. Tiffany screamed. The cop turned to fire at her but she threw herself back on the floor and fired at him. She shot him once in the groin and when he crouched over from reflex, she shot him in the head.

"Oh my God!" Tiffany panicked as she scurried over to D-Ball. "Dante…" she said as she slapped his face. She leaned close to his mouth and could still hear him breathing. She lifted his shirt up and checked his vest. There was no blood so she slapped him a little harder. "Dante!" she said more hastily. D-Ball's eyes fluttered and then opened. He gasped for breath and then stuck his hand in his vest to ease the pressure he felt against his chest. He took a couple of deep breaths and then shook his head to shake off how disoriented he felt. Tiffany helped him stand up and they made their way down the hall. D-Ball felt like he couldn't breathe and didn't want to hold Tiffany back so he pulled away from her so he could lean against the wall and catch his breath.

"Go," he told her as he coughed.

"What about you?" Tiffany asked, frightened.

"I'm good, I just need a minute. It should only be one more hallway, which means Jamal isn't too far and more than likely Andre already found him. Go, I'm right behind you, I promise." D-Ball said to her as he leaned on his knees and took a deep breath.

Tiffany looked at him for a moment and then backed away. She cautiously made her way down the hallway and turned the corner. There was only one room left and the door was open. She could hear a scuffle inside as if someone was fighting. She closed her eyes and took a deep breath before making her way over to the door. When she got to the doorway, she saw Andre was fighting Kristoff and Jamal was fighting another guy who had him on the ground in some kind of leg lock. Tiffany breathed heavily as she watched, not sure what she should do. Just as she thought she should try to take a shot at the guy Jamal was fighting, the same officer who stabbed Pete crept up behind her. Jamal saw her when it happened.

"Tiffany!" he yelled at her. But it was too late. The cop stabbed Tiffany in her side and she dropped her gun. Her face contorted in pain and she screamed out. The room suddenly became hot. Tiffany whirled around and elbowed her attacker in the face as hard as she could. She elbowed him again and then kicked his knee cap just as she did the other cop in the apartment. When the cop started to fall backwards, she snatched his gun from his holster and shot him twice in the chest and once in the head. She breathed deeply as she dropped the gun and reached for the knife in her side but another cop came for her. He put her in a bear hug and squeezed her tight as if he intended to break her back. Tiffany frowned in pain. She grabbed his head and pushed her thumbs in his eyes. He snarled and pulled his head away, squeezing her tighter. Tiffany squealed loudly. She reached for the knife in her side and as painful as it was, she pulled it out and plunged it in the side of the guy's neck. He looked at her with wide eyes and she could hear him gargling on his blood. She grimaced against her own pain but partially smiled at his as she drove the knife in deeper until his gargling ceased and he fell to the floor. Tiffany took two steps back and then collapsed.

"Tiff!" Jamal yelled.

"Jamal…" Tiffany murmured. She fought to keep her eyes opened, but darkness began to take over.

Yani

18

When Andre set off the M-80, he quickly began dishing out head shots like the trained assassin he was. He moved quick and with accuracy. His only focus was to get to his son before anything happened to him. Even when he was shot in the bullet proof vest, he did not falter. He made it to a room where the door was closed and was sure Jamal was in there. He dumped his clip, put a fresh one in and chambered a round. While aiming at the door, he twisted the door knob carefully but waited a moment before opening. He stood off to the side and pushed the door open quickly. Just as he suspected, someone fired out of the door.

"Kristoff!" Andre yelled. "You wanted me all this time. Is your bitch-ass gonna shoot me like a pussy or fight me like a man?" Andre taunted. He put his hands up with his gun in the air and slowly turned the corner. He saw that Kristoff had a gun to Jamal's head and Jamal was on his knees. Andre looked at his son and then looked at Kristoff. "You wanted me, muthafucka, you got me. Let my son go," Andre said calmly.

"You killed my son. It's only right that I kill yours," Kristoff said with malice.

"You killed my fucking brother and my nephew. You shot my wife and you're bitching to me about one little brat?" Andre said with a grimace.

Kristoff pushed the gun closer to Jamal's head and Jamal closed his eyes for a moment before looking up at his father. "I'ma make you eat those fucking words. Let's see how you feel when I have you watch as I blow your son's fucking brains out."

"No!" Andre yelled. "You want me, muthafucka. So bring your bitch-ass over here and come get me. Man to man, once and for all, you wetback, monkey-ass muthafucka!" Andre knelt down and sat his gun on the floor and then stood up slowly.

Kristoff hit Jamal in the face with the butt of the gun making him fall to the floor He then sat his gun on the metal table and rolled up his sleeves. "I'm going to beat your nigger-ass to fucking death. And then I'm still going to kill your fucking son, just like I killed your brother," Kristoff said as he threw his hands up. He advanced to Andre and swung. Andre dipped back and ducked before hitting Kristoff in the ribs. He wrapped his arms around his back and rushed him towards the metal table. Kristoff elbowed Andre hard in the center of his back twice and then kneed him in his stomach. Andre stumbled back and Kristoff hit him with a right hook.

Jamal scurried to his feet and rushed Kristoff, giving him three kidney punches. Kristoff tried to elbow Jamal, but Jamal ducked and upper cut him in the ribs. He then grabbed him by the neck and punched him in the eye. Kristoff grabbed onto Jamal and they slung each other around. Out of nowhere, another guy came and punched Jamal in the head. Andre snatched Kristoff off of his son and they began to box, with Andre whipping Kristoff's ass like he stole something. Jamal's opponent wrestled him more so than boxed him, but Jamal fought back better than he was expected to. Jamal managed to break his opponent's nose right before he was foot swept and knocked to the floor. Jamal grabbed for his opponent's leg and pulled him to the floor also. Somehow, Jamal found himself on the end of a fierce leg lock. He tried multiple ways to free himself but couldn't break free. He happened to look towards the door and saw Tiffany standing there looking terrified.

He then saw the same cop who stabbed Pete in front of him, appear behind Tiffany.

"Tiffany!" Jamal yelled out just as the cop stabbed her in her side. Jamal saw the way her body tensed up on an angle and the way her face frowned in pain. Her screams awakened a fury in him like none he had felt since Tamera had been killed. He struggled to get away from his opponent so he could get to his girlfriend. As a last resort, Jamal grabbed his opponent's genitals and squeezed unmercifully. The man jerked away and Jamal swung his foot around, kicking him in the mouth and jaw. When he fell back, Jamal jumped up and ran around the back of him. He placed one hand on the side of the man's head and his other hand on the opposite side of his face near his jaw and broke his neck. He pushed his opponent to the floor and looked up towards where Tiffany was. He saw when she plunged the knife that was previously in her side into the guy's neck as he held her in a tight bear hug. The guy let her go and collapsed onto the floor. Tiffany took two staggering steps back and then collapsed on the floor as well.

"Tiff!" Jamal yelled out to her as he got to his feet. He was about to make his way over to her when he heard two gun shots. Jamal jumped and then turned to see Kristoff standing over his father. He had shot him twice in the chest. His father was not moving.

"NO!" Jamal yelled. Kristoff turned his gun on Jamal. Jamal trembled as he looked down at his father who lay very still. He then turned his cold eyes onto Kristoff.

"Revenge never tasted so fucking sweet," Kristoff said as he aimed his gun at Jamal's head. He was about to squeeze the trigger when he saw movement behind Jamal. He looked only to see Tiffany aiming her gun at him. She fired once, hitting him in the throat. Jamal flinched and whirled around. She fired again, hitting Kristoff in the chest, putting him down. She whimpered and then dropped her gun as she lay on the floor.

Jamal looked at Kristoff and then looked at his father. He hurried over to Tiffany.

"Tiff…Tiff…" Jamal said as he got on his knees next to her. His eyes teared up as he pulled Tiffany in his arms, crying. He rocked her and smoothed her hair out of her face. "Baby, hold on. Hold on," he said as he continued to rock her. Tiffany looked up at him in too much pain to say anything. She shook her head as she held onto his shirt tightly.

"I know, babe. I know. Just hold on okay, please. For me, Tiff hold on," Jamal begged. "DANTE!" he cried out. He looked down at Tiffany and shook his head. He could hear her whimpering as she clung to his shirt. Her eyes fluttered as they began to close. Jamal shook her. "No Tiff! Open your eyes, babe. Open your eyes!" He gently tapped her on her face.

D-Ball appeared in the doorway. He looked down at Tiffany in Jamal's arms and his heart sank into his stomach. He then looked over at Andre and Kristoff.

"Call the ambulance, Dante! Call somebody." Jamal begged his friend. D-Ball reached in his pocket and pulled out his cell-phone. He called it in and then went over to Andre. He checked his pulse and saw that not only did he have one, but it was a very strong one. D-Ball wondered how that was possible with all of the blood coming from his torso. He tapped Andre's face with the back of his hand and Andre jerked his eyes open.

"Shit," he groaned. "Muthafucka shot me."

"What...the hell?" D-Ball said as he looked Andre over.

Andre used his elbows to sit up and tapped his vest. "Modern day technology; gotta fuckin' love it." D-Ball helped him stand up and Andre limped over to Kristoff. He bent over and picked up his gun.

"Do svidaniya," he said maliciously as he aimed at Kristoff's head. He fired another shot, just to be sure. He then looked at D-Ball. "History repeats itself for all those who forgot it. I ain't trying to have that muthafucka come back from the dead again." He arched his back and groaned. "I'm too old for this shit."

Rather than wait for the ambulance to get there, they helped Jamal carry Tiffany to the Range Rover and they quickly drove her to the hospital. Jamal hoped that history didn't repeat itself and he prayed that Tiffany survived.

18

Five months passed since the violent day in Kristoff's basement. With all of the surveillance Andre had along with the information that Pete's father had been compiling over the years, not only was Andre able to help Jamal bring down the cops, sergeants, lieutenants, captains and other corrupt officials in Philly as well as Delaware and New Jersey, but in exchange for all the information Andre had, he was exonerated and given full immunity for his past indiscretions. Finally Jamal would be able to have his father in his life without fear that he would have to dodge bullets or evade arrest.

Jamal and D-Ball were also given promotions for their hard work that resulted in the many indictments and sentencing of the corrupt officers. It pissed Bradley off as he did not like having to answer to Jamal. Jamal loved his new position and loved getting under Bradley's skin every chance he got.

ATR 3: The Wrath of Andre

He was lying across the bed in his new apartment watching ESPN as usual, happy to see that Shawn was drafted to the Miami Heat and would be playing alongside Lebron James and Dwyane Wade. He knew a championship ring would be in his brother's immediate future.

Tiffany came into the bedroom and climbed on Jamal's back. She leaned over and kissed his ear. "Baby, I've got a surprise for you," she whispered in his ear.

"What's that?" he asked as he turned his head to the side so he could see her.

Tiffany grinned and then handed him a pregnancy test that showed a blue plus sign. Jamal took it from her and looked at it wide eyed.

"For real?!" Jamal asked.

"Yes," Tiffany nodded with a smile.

"Seriously?!" Jamal asked again.

"Yes!" Tiffany replied.

Jamal turned over and sat up underneath her. He wrapped his arms around her and kissed her longingly. "YOOOO!! I'ma be a father!!" he exclaimed excitedly. He kissed her again and hugged her. He rubbed his hands over her neck and leaned his forehead against hers. "I love you, babe."

Yani

"I love you, too…daddy," Tiffany giggled. Jamal chuckled and kissed her again.

Two weeks after Jamal and Tiffany found out they would be expecting their first child together; Chanda, Deisha, Keisha and Tiffany were in a room together at Mt. Airy Baptist Church. Chanda was getting ready for her wedding with Shawn. The ladies were photographed as they helped Chanda with her make-up and accessories. Her wedding gown was strapless with white pearls embedded around the cleavage of the dress flowing down the front in an elegant design and then around the hem before it stopped at the second half of her dress which was made of fine Italian silk with the bottom back half sewn in a design that resembled multiple white roses all the way back to her four foot train. She wore diamond chandelier earrings with a matching necklace and tiara. Chanda looked like a beautiful Black Princess ready to marry her Prince and the love of her life.

"You look beautiful," Deisha said to her friend as she lightly hugged her from behind, making sure to not mess up their make-up.

"Thank you," Chanda gushed. "Oh my God. This was like a fantasy of mine back in the tenth grade. I never imagined that Shawn Williams would one day be my husband."

"And ya baby daddy," Keisha said in her best ghetto girl accent. The girls giggled.

"How did the two of you meet?" Tiffany asked.

Chanda smiled, "I knew him since the second grade but I've been in love with him since the eighth. One day, me and Deisha and our friend Tamera were walking down the street…" Chanda began to reflect back on the day that she found out Shawn liked her just as much as she had liked him.

"Deisha, you can barely keep up with your man because he's forever sniffing around Jamal. And Chanda…" Tamera said as she looked her friend up and down distastefully. "…you don't even have a man…"

"And the look on Tammy's face when she said that to me was soooo funny!" Chanda said as her and Deisha cracked up laughing.

"Yesss!" Deisha chimed in. "So then…" Deisha added on as she too thought back to that day.

"Be quiet 'cause from I hear, Shawn likes her," Deisha said.

"Shawn?!" Chanda exclaimed.

"Shawn Williams? Basketball Shawn?" Tamera chimed in.

"Yup!" Deisha said as she nodded her head.

"That can't be right because Trice told me that Shawn wasn't worried about no girls because all he was concerned about was basketball and getting into Temple." Chanda said replaying the information that she pumped from one of the cheerleaders.

Deisha burst out laughing. "Trice was lying her lil' butt off."

"Right! She was trying to be smart because she wanted to talk to Shawn but he ain't want her. Stupid chick didn't even know he always wanted to be a Hoya. He ain't wanna go to no damn, Temple." The girls laughed together.

"Wow, y'all taking me back down memory lane with this. I still remember that day. We were trying hard to keep Tammy from hooking up with Jamal back then," Deisha said as she thought back to their friend.

"How come?" Tiffany asked.

"Gurrrrl…Your lil boo used to be a lil thug in those streets," Chanda said.

"Every time you turned around his ass was in shit," Deisha and Chanda said at the same time. They laughed and slapped each other a high five. Tiffany and Keisha laughed with them

"Oh my God! Remember that time we were in the Gallery and that guy tried to talk to Tammy, and Jamal, Shawn and Maurice caught him?" Chanda asked Deisha.

"Ugh, don't remind me of that. Sometimes I still get pissed that Jamal smacked the shit outta me out there," Deisha rolled her eyes but started cracking up.

"What?! Jamal hit you?" Tiffany winced.

"Don't worry, he is far from a woman beater. It was just a lot of bad blood between me and him back then and you know what, I was kinda asking for that shit," Deisha explained.

"Why don't you let her arm go Jamal? Damn what the hell is wrong with you?" Deisha asked after marching over to Jamal and Tamera.

"Mind your business, Deisha," Tamera warned.

"No, he doesn't have any business gripping you up like you're a fucking man!" Deisha snapped.

Jamal released his hold on Tamera's arm and glared at Deisha. "You need to mind your business and shut the fuck up," he snapped at her.

"No, you shut the fuck up! Ain't nobody scared of your bitch-ass! You swear you're tough when you really ain't shit without your nut-ass cousin at your back."

Jamal smacked Deisha in her mouth, knocking her into a car...

"Oh my God, are you serious!?" Tiffany asked as she covered her mouth to suppress her giggle.

Deisha nodded her head. "Yes baby. Maurice was about to fuck his ass up for that shit, too." Deisha and Chanda started cracking up laughing as they thought back to Maurice throwing Jamal on top of the car and challenging him.

"Y'all all cursing in a church," Keisha giggled as she shook her head.

"My bad, God gonna have to forgive me today," Chanda said as she dabbed the corners of her eyes with a napkin after they started to tear up from laughing. "Ay yo! What about that time Jamal whipped the dude ass in the movie theater because he bumped Tammy and made her spill all that juice on the front of her shirt?" she said with laughter.

ATR 3: The Wrath of Andre

"Yes! Tiff, one thing you ain't gotta worry about with Jamal is him ever letting anybody disrespect you because he will knock a nigga smooth the fuck out," Deisha said as she smiled at Tiffany.

"Yes baby, like on the balcony at Uni! He whipped bol ass for calling Tammy a bitch!" Chanda hollered.

Deisha clapped her hands and stomped her feet as she laughed. "Yessss!! Oh my God! We had so much fun in Uni. I'm so sad that they closed our school down this year."

"I know right," Keisha replied.

Deisha looked at Keisha as she put on a pair of earrings. "Wow, I remember when you were a little freshman trying to hang with us." Keisha smiled at Deisha.

"Nah, I remember when we were coming home and those dingy chicks were jumping you," Chanda said.

"Girl, the way you jumped out of Shawn's car before he had a chance to stop and hauled ass over to the fight…!!!" Deisha replied.

"What the hell is going on now?" Deisha asked as she peeped out of the window.

Yani

Chanda noticed Keisha swinging frantically on the girls and jumped out of the car.

"Where are you going?" Shawn hollered as he stopped the car.

Chanda snatched off her heels and her earrings. "They're jumping your sister, Maurice!" She took off running to the fight with Maurice and Deisha running behind her. She wasted no time when she got over there. She hit one girl with her shoe and punched another girl in her face. Deisha followed up..."

The girls burst out laughing. "Damn straight, because we ride for ours," Chanda giggled.

"Wow, Danielle, Brandy and those other two chicks. I heard Brandy was killed by her boyfriend a couple years ago," Keisha said.

"Seriously?!" Deisha said with her mouth gaped open.

Keisha nodded her head. "Yup."

"So how long have you and Maurice been together?" Tiffany asked Deisha.

"Since February of '99." Deisha said proudly with a smile.

"Wow! Really!" Tiffany said with wide eyes.

"Yeah. We had been friends since we were in elementary school. Then my boyfriend Raheem was

258

killed summer of '98. Him, Maurice, Jamal and Shawn were real close. They killed him right in front of Jamal." They fell silent as Deisha and Chanda thought back to that day. Deisha cleared her throat and blinked back tears that threatened to fall. "But that shit had me so messed up because I was already going through crap at home with my mom and my aunt was fighting to get custody of me. Raheem was like the only good thing I had at the time. When he got killed, I remember I went off on Jamal. I blamed him for so long for Raheem's murder not even realizing how that shit messed with his head. I remember Maurice pulled me away and walked me home and I was in the bathroom puking my heart out. He just kept rubbing my back and when I calmed down, he went to the store and bought me a ginger-ale and a bag of Spicy Nacho Doritos," Deisha smiled as she remembered that small detail. "I laid my head in his lap and he just kept running his fingers through my hair until I fell asleep. I think my aunt let him stay the night that night because every time he tried to get up, I kept clinging to him."

"Awww," Tiffany and Keisha said at the same time. "That definitely is love." Tiffany said.

"Yeah, he came over every day after that and sat with me, walked with me to the funeral, sat with me through it and just been there ever since," Deisha smiled.

"Yes, this is the only woman for my brother," Keisha gushed.

"Y'all never broke up?" Tiffany asked.

"We had our little spats like most couples do. We broke up in 2010…" Deisha shook her head as she thought back to that day.

Deisha sat on the side of the bed in her and Maurice's one bedroom apartment in the Fern Rock section of Philadelphia. She was nervous and frightened at the same time as she waited for Maurice to come in from work. She heard the door open and close and moments later he came into the bedroom.

"Hey babe," Maurice greeted her with a kiss. Deisha stared at the floor holding an envelope in her hands. "How was your day?"

Deisha shook her head and wiped her face. Maurice hung his jacket up and then looked at her when he noticed her silence. He sat on the bed next to her.

"What's up?" Maurice asked as he ran his fingers through her hair. Deisha turned to look at him but couldn't form the words. Instead she handed him the envelope and put

her hands to her face. Maurice looked at her puzzled and then opened the envelope. He looked over the paperwork recognizing it as something from the doctors. When he saw that the paper work stated Deisha was pregnant, he became excited. But then his smile faded when he saw that the pregnancy was terminated.

"Are you fucking serious? Are you fucking serious?!" Maurice exclaimed as he stood up. "You were pregnant?"

Deisha kept her hands over her face in part to hide her tears and in part to keep from seeing the disappointment and anger in his face.

"You've gotta be fucking kidding me! How the fuck…" Maurice couldn't even find the words. "Why didn't you tell me? Why would you just go behind my back and fucking kill my child without even asking for my input?!"

"It's my body!" Deisha exclaimed and Maurice saw that she had been crying.

"But you didn't even give me a chance! You didn't even give me any say. It was my baby, too!" Maurice threw the paperwork and put his hands to his face. He was angry, frustrated and almost in tears as well. "Twelve years, Deisha! Twelve fucking years and you still don't trust me! You still don't trust us!"

"I do trust you!" Deisha replied. "But I'm not ready…"

"*You act like you would've been by yourself with this shit. I'm busting my ass to take care of everything now because I know how bad you wanted your Master's degree. So why the fuck couldn't you trust that I would've taken care of you and the baby? Aw damn, Deisha!*" *Maurice exclaimed as he turned his back with his hands to his head.*

"I'm sorry, Maurice…" Deisha said as she began to feel horrible about her hasty decision. She was extremely emotional and in fear that she would turn out like her mother, something that she never expressed to him, but the main reason behind her decision to terminate the pregnancy. She looked down at the ring on her finger that he had given to her just a couple of weeks before when he proposed. She slid it off her finger and then walked over to the dresser. "I'm so sorry…" she said as she sat her ring on the dresser along with her keys to their apartment. Maurice looked down at them and then looked at her but she couldn't meet his gaze.

"You can't even look at me right now," Maurice said to her. He sniffed as he waited for her to say something. Deisha shook her head and made her way to the door. "If you leave Deisha, don't bother coming back. This ain't high-school and we're not kids or teenagers anymore. If you can't be a woman and deal with this like a woman should, don't come back."

Deisha stopped for a moment afraid to leave, afraid to walk away from Maurice but more afraid of being a carbon

262

copy of her mother. She opened the door to their apartment and closed it quietly behind her as she left.

The girls were quiet as Deisha played with her nails.

"But it was meant to be because y'all found y'all way back to each other," Keisha said as she rubbed Deisha's back. "And y'all have a beautiful son."

"Yes, y'all do." Chanda chimed in.

"So when are you and Jamal getting married?" Deisha asked Tiffany with a smile.

Tiffany gagged and then coughed. "Oh…we haven't talked about it," she said nervously.

"Well the two of you are great together. I haven't seen Jamal this in love since Tammy and prior to that Jamal didn't love anything except money and the streets," Deisha said. Chanda nodded her head in agreement as she smoothed a fly away hair back in place.

Tiffany blushed and shook her head. "We just found out we're expecting."

The girl's squealed excitedly before gathering around and groping Tiffany.

"Wow, how far along are you?" Chanda asked.

"Only seven weeks. But he was so excited when I told him," Tiffany replied with a huge grin.

"Jamal is going to make an awesome father," Keisha smiled. A knock went at the door.

"Come in," Chanda said as she stood up.

Chanda's father and Jamal came in. Chanda shrieked and ducked behind Deisha. "Jamal, get out! You ain't slick, you're trying to tell Shawn what I look like!" she giggled.

"I just came to give my sis-n-law a hug and say congrats since you're about to walk down the aisle," Jamal said as he came over to her and gave her a hug. "You look beautiful."

"Thank you, Jamal," Chanda beamed.

Jamal looked at Tiffany and winked at her. Tiffany blushed and smiled back at him. Deisha looked at both of them and smiled.

"Daddy!" Chanda said as she hugged her father.

"Look at you, looking just like your grandmother. You look beautiful," Tyrone told his daughter.

"Thank you, Daddy. I wish mom and Kareem could be here to see me," Chanda said as she swallowed back her tears. Carmen passed away suddenly from a brain aneurysm while Chanda was in Italy pregnant with Amber.

"They're looking down on you, so proud and so happy for you." Tyrone told his daughter as he kissed her forehead. Chanda nodded unable to fight back her tears any longer. Deisha grabbed a napkin and wiped the corner of her eyes and then hugged her.

The photographer came in and took more photos of them and then got photos of the groom and his groomsmen.

"Places everyone," Deisha said. Keisha stood in front so she could walk down the aisle with D-Ball. Behind her was Tiffany who was going to be walking down with Jamal and behind her was Deisha who was walking down with Maurice. Chanda's son Dre was the ring bearer and lastly was Chanda's younger sister and her daughter Amber as the flower girls. The music began, starting with N'Sync's *This I Promise You.*

When it came time for Chanda to walk down the aisle, the music changed to Jesse Powell's *You.*

"That's your cue, sweetheart," Tyrone said as he looked at his daughter. "You ready?"

Chanda nodded. "Just don't let me fall," she giggled nervously.

Tyrone chuckled with her and the doors opened. Everyone stood up as Tyrone and Chanda slowly made their way down the aisle. When Chanda saw Shawn in his tuxedo, she became visibly shaken. Her heart fluttered as she kept her eyes on him and it took everything in her body to keep from running to him. She thought back to all of their tender moments together from the start of their relationship until that moment. The first time they made love, the first time he told her he loved her, the way he cared for her when her brother was murdered right in front of her. She smiled as she remembered seeing him cry during the birth of their son Andre and as he cut the umbilical cord. Shawn was the love of her life, the only man for her and today she was going to vow to spend the rest of her life with him.

Shawn stood next to his older brother and watched Chanda as she made her way down the aisle. His thoughts were similar to hers as he thought back on all of their years together and how much he loved her. He extended his hand to her when she made it down the aisle and her father gave her to him. Tyrone shook Shawn's hand and kissed Chanda on the cheek.

Chanda was so nervous and happy that her whole body shook as if she were shivering while the

Pastor presided over them. They stared into each other's eyes, smiling as if they were the only ones in the church. After saying their vows and placing their rings on each other's fingers, they were pronounced husband and wife.

"You may now kiss your bride," the pastor told them.

Shawn pulled Chanda close to him by her hand and kissed her longingly. "I love you," he said before kissing her again.

"I love you," Chanda replied as she kissed him back.

The guests cheered as the pastor introduced them. "Ladies and gentlemen, allow me to introduce Mr. and Mrs. Williams. What God has joined together, let no man put asunder."

Shawn and Chanda held hands and walked down the aisle with the wedding party following behind them.

At the reception, Jamal tapped on the wine glass so he could make a speech.

"Good evening, everyone. I was going to bust out with a freestyle for old time sake," Jamal chuckled. The guests laughed along with him. "Nah, I'm not gonna embarrass myself like that. I look around at everyone here, new faces, old faces; and I think of those who aren't here with us, those who we lost over the years. My brother and I went through so much over the last fifteen years but the one constant good thing through the most of those years has been his wife, Chanda. While a lot of people look at Beyoncé and Jay-Z or Kanye and Kim and see them as power couples and look up to them, these two are truly a power couple. Through so many storms, so many trials and tribulations, so much loss, so much pain, they stayed together. They weren't just boyfriend and girlfriend, but they were and still are best friends. They inspired me and I'm un-inspirable. There is absolutely no better woman in this world for my brother." Jamal turned to his new sister-in-law. "Chanda, you are the definition of a strong Black woman. You are what every Black man needs and you are everything my brother deserves. I wish y'all nothing but peace, happiness and all the love your hands and hearts can hold," Jamal smiled at his brother and his new wife as he raised his glass. "Salute with me y'all. To the bride and groom."

After everyone toasted and enjoyed their meal, Chanda and her father danced to Beyoncé's song *Daddy*.

ATR 3: The Wrath of Andre

Andre made his way over to Shawn and shook his hand. "Congrats son," he said to him.

"Thanks, Dad," Shawn replied. Keyona walked over to them and had Jamal, Andre and Shawn stand together to get a picture of them.

Shawn and Chanda took to the floor for their solo dance together, dancing to Eric Benet and Tamia's *Spend my Life*. Jamal watched them, feeling proud of his younger brother. He thought back to their childhood, playing basketball together in the streets with a crate nailed to a wooden pole, posing as a basketball hoop. He remembered when Shawn was the best freestyler in the neighborhood and thought back to how they both hung on the corner of 26th and Bailey Street with Raheem and Maurice. He smiled as he thought back to their days in high school hanging in the lunchroom laughing and talking. They both came a long way and this was the first time in a long time that Jamal felt at peace.

Shawn looked at Jamal and gave him a smile and a nod. Jamal nodded back at him and then thought of Tamera. He closed his eyes as he thought back to their last moments together and when she finally told him she loved him. He opened his eyes and looked around for Tiffany. He saw her coming back from the bathroom and could tell by the look on her face and the way she wiped her mouth in a napkin that morning sickness had attacked her. He stared at her lovingly and then touched the ring around his neck. He looked down at it as he played with it between his fingers.

"Thank you for watching over me, Tammy. I'll always love you…" Jamal thought to himself. He reached behind his neck and unfastened the chain that the ring hung from and held it in his hand. He kissed the ring one last time and then tucked it in his pocket. He happened to look at Deisha who raised her glass to him as if to salute him after she saw what he did with the ring, reminding her of when she finally took Raheem's chain off. Jamal raised his glass at her in return and then looked back at Tiffany. She was staring at him smiling. He smiled back and mouthed, "I love you."

Tiffany smiled at him and blew him a kiss. "I love you, too," she mouthed back.

Thug Redeemed!!

1

Markel

The sound of my alarm clock screeching like a freight train straining to come to a halt blared in my ears and snatched me out of my dream which was actually a pretty good one. I was back in my undergrad days living the good and wild life, getting any lady I wanted, being a pimp, hated by the brothers that wished they could be me and loved and lust after by the women that wished they could get a taste of the mojo I was always laying on them. Ahh yes, I was indeed the definition of a player. But now those days are dead and gone and I am a one woman man. My wife, my boo, my right hand lady Tierra has stayed with me in spite of all of my in-discretions. Sometimes I wonder if she knew about all of the cheating and the double life I was leading with her and my side "jawns" and just kept her mouth closed. Maybe she even got a little on the side. No, I'm not going to think that. Even though I did my dirt I don't even want to think of the possibility of another man running up in my wife. I would have to murder something.

Now I'm looking at her sleeping beside me. Damn, she is truly beautiful. No matter how many women I had that would have done anything-and I do mean anything- to be with me, I knew it was only because I was popular and they smelled success. Those bitches were just trying to hitch on and get a free ride. Tierra, she was real. She was loyal. And still is. She is the definition of what a 100 percent woman truly is supposed to be: smart, beautiful, a great conversationalist, and a great cook. I mean my baby can really throw down. She has her own catering business and was just contracted to do a cook book as well as do a cooking segment on Rachel Ray's Morning Show. Yes, my baby is the bomb diggity. Did I mention this woman has some toe curling cuddy? After almost 16 years, this woman still manages to surprise me in bed and leave me glowing like a newly fucked virgin, grinning from ear to ear, drooling, and wondering all at the same time, DAMN!!! Where the hell did she learn how to do that?! And to think I almost screwed everything up with her, running around, sticking and moving with a bunch of smuts that didn't have half of what Tierra has. I'm just looking at her right now laying on her side, back arched, silk sheets, clinging to her curvy body outlining that sexy frame that still looks tight after giving birth to our three beautiful kids. Damn, the way that ass of hers is pointing in my direction is making me want to slob her down right now. Damn, my baby is fine! I love her to death. I really don't know what I would do without her.

I can hear the kids up. It sounds like Tamia and Tianna are going at it again. Those girls stay going at it. And here comes one knocking on the door.

"Daddy!!" That was Tianna. She's ten years old but is such a Tom-boy and swears she's a little boxer, though I must admit, she has a mean right hook and has made me want to cry uncle when she punched me in my damn eye. I was almost ready to whip her little ass.

"Yes sweetheart," I replied placing my hands behind my head knowing what was coming next.

Without getting permission from me, Tianna burst open my door, marched into my bedroom, and placed her hand on her tiny hips taking a defiant stance. That was her, "I'm sick of this shit" pose. I managed to suppress my chuckle and asked her what was wrong.

She rolled her eyes and started tapping her foot. I almost cracked up. "Tamia has been in the shower for the last half hour washing her hair AGAIN, and I have to go to the bathroom."

Now I had to roll my eyes. Tamia. That girl. Every time I turn around she is taking forever in the damn day to get herself ready in the morning. She just turned thirteen and thinks she is miss body beautiful. She has long medium brown hair just like her mother. The same almond shaped baby brown eyes, thick, naturally arched eye brows, long lashes and smooth sandy brown skin. And unfortunately, puberty has begun to kick in a little sooner than I would have liked because she has to be sporting at least a 34B with a little tiny waste and a little apple bottom. As her father, I naturally am ready to pull a Martin Lawrence from Bad Boys 2 and intimidate any little nucca that thinks he is going to smooth talk his way into my baby girl's pants. I was thirteen once, too. And I can't even begin to tell you the filthy thoughts that would have been running through my mind had Tamia grown up with me and my little crew of cronies. Yeah … I definitely was going to be keeping a hawk eye on her.

Yani

I guess I didn't answer her fast enough because Tianna started tapping her foot louder.

"Daddy, did you hear me?" she asked impatiently. "Tell her to get out of the bathroom. I gotta go!" She crossed her legs and started doing the "pee-pee" dance to drive her point home. I got out of the bed and let her use our master bathroom and then decided to handle Miss America.

I tapped on the bathroom door.

"I said wait, DANG!!" Tamia hollered from behind the door.

"Who the hell do you think you're talking to like that?" I shouted back. I heard her wince behind the door.

"Sorry, Daddy. I thought you were Tianna again. She's knows I'm in here trying to get ready for school."

I could just see her rolling her eyes while she did whatever the hell it was that she was doing to her head. "Regardless who you thought it was, you don't yell in my house. Get your little scrawny ass out the bathroom. You're not the only one that has to go to school." I could hear her suck her teeth and snatch her things up in the bathroom. Though her words weren't exactly audible, I knew she was talking shit.

"You say something?"

"No, Daddy," she mumbled. Yeah, she knows who the boss is. She cracked the door open and peeked out. I scanned over her and noticed how unusually short her uniform skirt was. I shook my head. You can't even send your kids to Catholic School to keep them in line. They always gotta push the envelope...even with Jesus.

"What the hell is wrong with your skirt?" I asked her.

She looked down at herself and gave me the dumb blonde look like she had no idea what I was talking about. "What do you mean?" she asked with wide innocent eyes.

"Where is the rest of it?"

She chuckled and threw her hand on my chest. "Dad, you're silly."

"You see me damn it laughing? Ether you have Tianna's uniform on or you need to pull your skirt down. Either way, don't play yourself. Pull that damn skirt down."

She sulked past me and whined, "Aww Dad, come on. It's not even that high. It looks corny all the way past my knees."

"Yeah and you look like Steve Urkel with the

hem of your skirt around your collar bone. Pull that damn skirt down." I could tell she was embarrassed by my last comment. But oh well. She pulled her skirt down and pulled her knee highs up before sulking towards her bedroom. "And put your hair in a ponytail. And don't even think about pulling your skirt back up when you get to school. I got eyes everywhere. So even when you think I'm not looking, I still see you." I heard Tianna skipping down the hallway behind me.

"Ah ha!" she teased. "That's what you get for trying to be cute for them nappy-headed knuckle-heads that hang around the building in the morning and in the afternoon. Daddy, Tamia's trying to get a boyfriend." She leaned into the wall laughing and slapped her knee.

"Shut up Tianna!" Tamia screamed from her bedroom.

"Who's the knuckle-head, Tee-Tee?" I asked my younger daughter chuckling with her.

"His name is Troy and he's ugmo," she whispered in between her laughs. I laughed out loud with her. Ugmo? Damn. My little girl was getting dolled up for a troll. Her mom was definitely going to have to school her.

Tamia snatched her door open. "You talk too much you little troll. I am not trying to get a boyfriend. I don't even like Troy. You need to mind your business."

"Hey, what did I just tell you about your mouth? You better chill real quick with your lip Tamia or the only thing you'll be kissing is the back of your momma's hand." She closed her mouth quickly knowing Tierra did not play when it came to sassy-mouthed little girls. "Now I don't give a damn who Troy is but you better stay outta his face and I better not catch him in yours or I'll buss his ass and then I'ma buss yours. Don't let me hear anything else about you trying to wear your school uniform skirts a little shorter to get attention from some ugmo Negro." Tianna burst out laughing and Tamia rolled her eyes and crossed her arms over her chest. "And that goes for you too, Smoking Joe." That was a little nick name that I gave my younger daughter since she has such a mean right hook.

"You don't have to worry, Daddy. Boys are the last thing on my mind. They're immature, simple and don't know nothing about nothing."

"That's right." I agreed as I gave my daughter a pound. "Go get ready for school. And wake your little brother up, too." I went back in the bedroom and saw that Tierra wasn't in the bed anymore. So much for my early morning jump off. Damned rugrats. I went into our master bathroom that connected to our bedroom and saw that she was finishing brushing her teeth.

"Good morning, baby." I put my arms around her waist from behind and hugged her to me before kissing the side of her mouth. She turned her head a little to meet my mouth and gave me a big wet kiss. Then she handed me the toothpaste.

"Good morning, babe." She giggled. "Handle that."

"Oh, I see you got jokes early in the morning. You're trying to be funny." I snatched the toothpaste from her playfully.

"No I'm not. Your breath is just a little tart. That's not cute." She laughed out loud and made her way out of our bathroom. I slapped her on her ass playfully.

"Was that the girls going at it again?" Tierra asked from the bedroom as I was brushing my teeth.

I swished water around my mouth and then spat it in the toilet and flushed. "Yeah. We really need to do something about Tamia and her attitude. Her mouth is getting a little bit crazy in here and that bathroom situation is getting out of hand." I came in the bedroom and began taking my clothes out for work.

"I've told her about her mouth too many times. That girl's mouth is seriously about to get her a check that her ass can't cash."

I looked at my wife and laughed. I loved how she is such a lady with such an aggressive attitude and a foul mouth to match. "Well if her ass can't cash the checks, will your ass take some deposits?" We both laughed.

"You are so damned nasty. I'm going to cook breakfast. Are you eating here or picking something up on your way into the office?"

"I gotta pick Darnell up since his car is in the shop so we might just grab something on our way in." I watched my wife walk out of the bedroom and head downstairs. I really am a lucky man.

2

Tierra

Markel has no idea how freaking lucky he is. I love that man to death but he has not made it easy to do so. He has cheated, lied and Lord only knows what else during the duration of our relationship which goes all the way back to 8th grade at Wannamaker Junior High School. Most people would say that I was stupid for staying with him, that I was and still am too good to deal with the bullshit that he was putting me through. But Eve said it best in her song lyrics: Love is blind, and it will take over your mind. I love Markel with everything I have inside of me and even though those dingy bitches may have had him for a night or two, I have the ring, the house, the Range Rover, the money, the commitment and ultimately the man. All they have are memories and thoughts of what could've been but never was. Besides, while he was doing his dirt on the side, I had my little action, too. What's good for the goose is good for the damn gander and two can definitely play that game. As far as I can tell, Markel has been totally faithful since we had Tianna and got married. And so have I. He comes home on time, he calls when he is going to be late and he is totally devoted to making me and the kids happy as well as taking care of home. Besides, he would be a fool to fuck up now. My baby is the head Physical Therapist at one of the most prestigious clinics in the Tri-state area. He has treated numerous athletes from Allen Iverson to Ocho-Cinco. My baby is well known and even sought after. So of course he is paid out of the ass making a six figure salary. But, as the saying goes, Hell hath no fury like a woman scorned...without a pre-nup. So he definitely knows better now.

Markel and I met when I moved from Atlanta to Philadelphia in the fall of 1997 when we were in the 8th grade. He was a little knuckle-head mofo with a crew of cronies that swore they were the next best thing since sliced bread. The boys in the class were immediately on my top because of my southern accent, curvy teenaged body and long dark brown hair. But the females, those chicken-heads threw shade on me the moment my gorgeous ass walked through the door.

I will never forget my first initial encounter with Markel. I had only been in school for about two weeks when one of the chicken-heads in the class figured she would test my gangsta. We were at lunch and they were jealous because my mother always sent me to school not only looking fresh but with hot, home cooked food so I didn't have to eat the nasty school lunch. The boldest chicken-head tripped me as I was walking by sipping on my Pepsi and I stumbled spilling the Pepsi on the front of my new Ralph Lauren sweat suit. Markel stood on top of the lunch table, laughed and shouted, "Check mate!" Little Ms. Chicken-Head had a crush on Markel and didn't like the fact that he and his boys were always trying to holler at me in school, so I guess she thought she would get his attention by dissing me. I had something special for that ass. I picked my bottle of Pepsi up, threw it in the trash and a couple of her friends decided to instigate. I walked over to Little Miss Chicken-Head and she stood up. I think she was about to say something but the words never made it out of that heifer's mouth because I knocked the shit out of that bitch. When she fell into the lunch table, I grabbed a carton of milk and poured it in her hair and her face and beat that ass. I was daring one of her little crew of sluts to jump into it because they would have gotten some of the same. When security broke the fight up, Markel stood on top of the table over the girl and said in his best Chris Tucker/Smokey from the movie *Friday* voice: "YOU GOT KNOCKED THE FUCK OUT!!!" Reminiscing about that now almost has me cracking up at this sink as I'm fixing breakfast for my babies.

I sat in the councilor's office with an ice-pack on my hand more pissed off that I had just gotten that damn sweatsuit and the bitch made me spill Pepsi on it than the fact that I was about to be suspended and hadn't even been in the damn school for a month. Markel snuck into the councilor's office and just stood in front of me. I looked up at him and we stared each other down. As angry as I was, he actually made me blush. He must've known that he had me because he started grinning. That turned my smile into a grimace. He burst out laughing and said, "You gonna knock me out, too?"

"Boy, get out of my damn face." I snarled at him.

"Ooh you better watch your mouth. You're already in trouble," he replied sitting next to me.

"So what. That's what that little cow gets for trying to test me." I rubbed the ice pack across my fist.

Markel just stared me in my face like I was going to be on the next science test and he needed to study me. "You're accent is tight," he complimented.

I turned around and looked at him but quickly looked away. I never noticed how cute he was until that moment. "Thank you," I mumbled.

"So look right. My name is Charlie and I need a body guard. Will you be my Angel?" We both burst out laughing. That had to be the corniest but cutest line I had ever heard any guy use. I laughed so hard I almost forgot that I had messed up my new outfit and was about to be suspended. The Principal came into the office and looked at the both of us.

"Markel Davis if you don't get out of this office and make your way back to your last period class, you will find your tail on the end of one of these pink slips, too." The Principal chided. She called my boy by his first and last name so I knew he had made her acquaintance more than once.

"Alright Ms. Jackson, my whole Government though," he joked. The look that she gave him let him know that she was not in a joking mood. "Okay, I'm going. But Tierra is my study partner so I figured if she is getting suspended, I might as well get her contact information to make sure she don't fall behind in the school work. We're about to get a test soon and she already started here late."

"Damn this boy has game for days," I thought to myself.

The Principal looked at him and then looked at me. I shrugged my shoulders and took a pen out of my bag and a piece of paper out of my book. I knew why he really wanted my number but his suave nature was too much to resist. I scribbled my name and number down on the paper and gave it to him. He grinned like a cat that had just caught the canary and left the office. From that moment on, he was a constant thought on my mind. Little did I know, he would be the source of my heart ache, the father of my children, but also the love of my life.

3

Darnell

"Yo Bro! Let's go. You know Mondays are always crazy busy and we got clients coming in today!" Markel shouted out of his window. Dude was always trying to cock block. I was trying to crack on a little shorty that was on her way into IHOP as we were on our way out. Shorty was looking right with her tight fitted jeans and Gucci boots with the matching bag. Nails done, hair done, oh yeah she was fancy!

"Hold on dawg, I'm coming. Chill out!" I turned my attention back to the little honey dip and smiled. "He's just mad because he's on lock down and is missing out on the finer things in life like you," I smiled at her and gave her the once over look. She giggled and took out her Android phone and put my number in it. I put her number in my IPhone and told her I would give her a call tonight so we could go out for dinner and maybe the comedy club. Kevin Hart was in town and there was no way I was going to miss that. As she turned to walk away, I took a picture of her ass. It took everything I had inside of me to keep from hollering "DAMN!" I can't wait to hit that. I strolled back over to Markel's car. It glistened in the sunlight from being freshly washed and waxed. That 2012 Acura was the shit. He had mad bitches on his dick just because of the car. I still don't know why he sold out and got married. I mean don't get me wrong, Tierra is cool and all, but she was just a school jawn and he should've left it at that. The only reason she got the ring is because she fucked around and got pregnant TWICE. Two rugrats just aren't enough for me to wife a bitch. And I still say ole dawg needs to get a DNA test for at least the first two. Because I'm pretty sure she had niggas creeping on the low while they were in school. She just always struck me as the sneaky bitch.

I hopped in the whip and threw my shades on once he pulled off and the sun started blaring in my eyes. "Yo, you were definitely in the way for that shit. You saw me trying to get with the little honey dip."

Markel leaned back in his leather seat and whipped the wheel around a turn with one hand. "Man, you can crack on any honey you want to dawg, but when clients come in for a tour of the facility to do business, you know I like to get in early to make sure everybody's shit is on point. Last thing I want to see are sloppy desks with a bunch of paper work and shit and patient charts unorganized and not where they are supposed to be. As for your honey dip, you better check shorty's ID and make sure her shit's legit. Last thing I need is to have my right hand man getting hauled off in handcuffs at the job. Shit is not good for business." We both cracked up laughing.

"You trying to play me, dude. Naw, shorty is cool. She's definitely something kinda spectacular."

"Yeah alright." Markel replied stopping at a red light. "All I'm saying is, you're getting up there in that age. Don't you think it's time for you to settle down a bit? You can't be a pimp forever." Markel is my home boy but he gets on my fucking nerves trying to talk me into settling down and having a family.

"Look yo, everybody ain't meant to be all locked down with a wife, kids, big house with the picket fence and the two car garage. I like my shit just the way it is. When a bitch gets out of line, on to the next one. These hoes are just scandalous gold diggers looking for a nigga to sponsor them. Outside of a meal and a movie, they can't get shit from me. That settling down shit might have worked out for you, but that shit is definitely for the birds when it comes to me and how I like to do things."

Markel shook his head. I could tell he didn't agree with me, but hey, that was his business. "You keep thinking and acting the way you're acting and that's all you're going to keep coming across are a bunch of gold diggers and hoodrat smut jawns. You're not going to meet your wife in the club, dawg. That's all I'm saying. The reason you attract those kinda chicks is because of the places you're meeting them."

"Alright yo, everybody ain't meant to be like you and Tierra with y'all little fairytale life. I'm not looking for a wife so it's all good. So just drop it alright?" Markel nodded his head and turned his sound system up extra loud. Rick Ross was blasting through the system. I guess Markel felt so free to tell me what kind of woman I should get with and how I should settle down because he thought his little precious Tierra is perfect. I laughed to myself. If only he knew...

It all started our sophomore year of College at Widener University. It's funny how we all came up together; from John Wannamaker to Engineering and

Science and then Widener University. Me and Markel had always been tight ever since elementary school. We vowed to not only be best friends, but brothers also when my older brother got killed on 20th and Susquehanna during a drive-by shooting. Nothing was ever supposed to come between us; niggas, money and especially bitches. It seemed like a lot of that changed when Tierra came into play our eighth grade year of junior high school. I'm not going to front, shorty was the shit when she started at the school. She had the body of a grown woman at thirteen with those big ass titties and that fat ass. I guess it's true when they say women from down south are built better because baby girl's body was like that. I was going to holler at her. Markel knew I was feeling shorty. But he tried some ole slick shit when she was in the Principal's office after getting into a fight in the lunchroom and got her number. I didn't trip though, and I definitely wasn't going to beef with him over no bitch. So I didn't say shit, I just let them do their thing. I thought it was just going to be one of those school relationships that only lasted a couple of weeks, maybe a few months at best. But they were like fucking Will Smith and Jada Pinkett. She was at all of his basketball games, they hung out on the weekends watching sports and playing video games. We got to high school and they were still together! The crazy shit was, the nigga hadn't hit it yet. She wasn't giving up no pussy, no head; NOTHING! She claimed she was a virgin and wasn't ready yet, but I wasn't buying that shit. Not with a body like that. That's what all smut-ass hoes say. Quiet chicks are the nastiest, sneakiest and freakiest little bitches in all of the continental U-S of muthafuckin' A! Markel was doing her mad dirty, though. Fucking bitches behind her back. He never fucked bitches from the same school, he always fucked bitches from other high schools. He had old jawns giving him money and rides to school and picking him up but lying to her saying they were his cousins or aunts. That shit was crazy because she never said shit. Either she was dumb as hell and didn't know, or she knew but played her fucking part. He finally hit our junior year of high school and for a while he had stopped cheating on her. I mean that nigga really tried to be faithful to her especially when she got pregnant. But when we got to college and he saw how more experienced them college bitches were and how easy it was to fuck them white jawns, my man turned into a straight up hoe on the low. Tierra started figuring shit out when we were in our second year of college. Prank calls, silly emails, chicks writing love letters to him but leaving them in her door. She came crying to me one day but never said what exactly the problem was. She just kept saying she was tired. At the time I thought she was tired from the baby and trying to keep up with school, but naw, she was tired of that nigga doing her dirty. So I talked to her; tried to make her feel better about herself, gave her the usual cap up that niggas give when a hoe is feeling down. I will admit, the conversations and text messages that we would send each other had me feeling her all over again like back in eighth grade. One night, I swung by their little apartment when I knew Markel was with one of his little honey dips, and I beat that pussy up. I knocked that shit out real good and gave it to her just the way she wanted it knowing that if I did it right, I could hit it again and I did. The whole spring semester I waxed that ass. I almost convinced her to leave Markel for me. But she started giving me sob-ass stories about how much she loved him and how they had a family together.

"So you're saying you don't love me? I'm the one that's been here with you all this time while that nigga is out doing him with any other bitch he can get. I've been here for you. I've been more of a family to you and Tamia than him, so what do you mean?" I said to her one night after we had finished making love.

"I wish you would stop saying that. Markel is not cheating on me. He has never cheated on me and would never cheat on me. And I know you've been there. And I appreciate that, I really do. But I can't just leave Markel for you. How would that look, me leaving him for his best friend?" She looked at me for a second and then turned her back to me.

"Were you thinking about how it looked when you were fucking his best friend? So you're saying you can fuck his best friend behind his back but you can't be with me in his face. What the fuck type shit is that?" I snapped. I couldn't believe she tried to hit me with that lame ass rationalization. Was she serious?

She whirled around with fire in her eyes and hit the shit out of me. Twice! She went to swing again and I grabbed her ass and slammed her into the bed. I pinned her down and screamed in her face. "Hoe, have you lost your muthafucking mind? Don't you ever put your fucking hands on me bitch, don't you know I will fuck you up in here?!"

She screamed back at me. "Get off me,

Yani

Darnell! Your punk-ass really gonna hit a woman? Get the fuck off of me!" She struggled to free herself. I guess she thought she was going to hit me again. I don't make idle threats.

"If you're tough enough to swing on a man be prepared to get your ass smacked the fuck back." We both stared at each other breathing like two wild animals about to battle in the jungle. She never looked sexier than she did at that moment; pissed off and ready to rumble. I pinned her arms above her head and kissed her hard and deep. I needed to remind her who Daddy was.

I turned her over on her side and put one leg up over my shoulder and slipped inside of her. She was still wet, slippery and sticky just the way I liked it. I thrust inside of her hard and deep and she moaned loudly and whispered my name.

"Don't get quiet now. Where's all that mouth now, huh?" I pushed her knee closer to her chest so I could go deeper. She cried out and started clawing the sheets. "Yeah that's right. This Daddy Dick, right here. You don't disrespect Daddy Dick, do you?"

Tierra moaned and replied, "No. I'm sorry. Please don't stop."

I turned her over so she was lying flat on her

296

stomach, legs straight with her ass arched just a little bit and I slipped back inside of her. I put my hands underneath her to cuff her titties and gave her long hard strokes. The pillow muffled her screams but I could hear her begging me to make her cum again. I stroked her as deep as I could until I felt her explode all over my dick. Feeling all of her hot, creamy wetness excited me and I bust inside of her. We laid there sweaty, and breathing heavy with her body wrapped in mine. Her little freak ass started tightening her pussy muscles around me. Women; no matter how much you knock it out the box, they just keep coming back for more. I rolled over next to her and pulled her close to me with my arms wrapped around her waist and my chin resting above her head. She locked her fingers into mine and with my free hand I stroked her long hair. Neither one of us said anything for a few moments. Nothing needed to be said. I knew I was wrong for what I was doing to my best friend. But evidently he didn't appreciate her with all of the dirt he was doing behind her back while she was taking care of their daughter, keeping their apartment together and making sure dinner was done when he got home, plus trying to keep up with college to get her degree. He didn't appreciate her strength or her beauty, but I did. I loved this woman. And even though they had a kid together and she wanted to keep her family, I knew that she loved me too. I just needed her to do the right thing.

I kissed her ear. "Babe, you still up?"

"Yeah, why?" she answered back in her afterglow voice.

"Look at me." She hesitated for a moment but then she turned and faced me but stared at my chest. "You know what we're doing is dead wrong, yo. Like, me and Mar been boys since way back when. That's my right hand man. He's like my brother. We've had each other's back through everything. I love him, yo. Blood couldn't make us any closer. But as much as you don't want to believe me, that nigga is doing you so dirty and you don't deserve that. You're too good for all of the shit that he is putting you through. You say he's not cheating on you but you're not stupid. You know. And I know you know what he's doing. What he's been doing. You holding that nigga down, playing your part, taking care of y'all daughter, taking care of home and going to school, yo. You're beautiful, smart, funny; you can get any man you want but you putting up with shit you don't deserve to be going through." A few tears slid out of her eyes and I wiped them away with my thumb.

"You might not believe me, but I love you, Tee. I would never do you the way he's doing you. Trust and believe that, shorty. We can't keep doing this, though. We either gonna have to tell him the truth or just stop all together. I don't want to lose you. But I don't want to keep playing this game either. I love you, yo."

That was the first time that I ever said fuck it and put myself, my heart, everything on the line for a female. She closed her eyes and let the tears fall. I wiped them away and kissed her. She pulled back and finally looked at me for a space of heartbeats.

"I can't." she whispered. "I can't leave him. And I can't tell him. I'm sorry, Darnell. I'm so sorry. But I can't."

My heart dropped into the pit of my stomach and shattered. But I wasn't going to give up. I loved this woman. And had Markel not pulled that slick shit to get her phone number, me and her would probably be together instead of us sneaking around behind his back. I slid from under the covers and started to get dressed. Fuck it, I could shower at my dorm. I left without saying goodbye and she didn't try to stop me.

About a month and a half later she found out

she was pregnant. I thought that would have made her leave Markel because I was positive that baby was mine. To this day, whenever I look at Tianna, I feel a connection to her. She reminds me so much of myself. She just looks identical to Tierra. She insisted the baby was not mine and broke it off with me. She changed her cell number and told Markel the reason being was because of too many solicitations from telemarketers. Next thing I know, four months into the pregnancy they were getting married. That's when I was pretty much done with the both of them. Those two frauding-ass bitches deserved each other. Ever since then, me and Markel's friendship hasn't been the same and to this day he still has no clue why. He just thinks it's because he settled down and I still choose to chase. So many times I wanted to put a bug in his ear but I ain't no snitch. So I said fuck it. No sense in me being stuck with a kid I wasn't ready for and even if I did snitch, what would I have gained? They would've broken up, me and Mar wouldn't be friends and she still wouldn't be with me. So yeah, fuck it. Ten years later and still no one is the wiser. But like the saying goes, what's done in the dark always comes to the light. And this bitch might think everything is gravy now. But sooner or later I will be there when the shit hits the fan and her perfect little world crumbles before her very eyes. I'll never chase another bitch again. I'm only after my paper. You can't trust these hoes. They are more scandalous and devious than the niggas…

Coming Soon to a Book Store Near You!!